CRAFTING A COLD CASE

Gasper's Cove Mysteries Book 6

BARBARA EMODI

Publisher: Amy Barrett-Daffin

Creative Director: Gailen Runge

Senior Editor: Roxane Cerda

Copy Editor: Second Glance Editorial

Cover Designer: Mariah Sinclair

Book Designer: April Mostek

Production Coordinator: Zinnia Heinzmann

Illustrator: Emilija Mihajlov

Published by C&T Publishing, Inc., P.O. Box 1456, Lafayette, CA 94549

Library of Congress Control Number: 2025936847

Printed in the USA

10 9 8 7 6 5 4 3 2 1

Gasper's Cove Mysteries Series

• Book 1 •
Crafting for Murder

• Book 2 •
Crafting Deception

• Book 3 •
Crafting with Slander

• Book 4 •
Crafting a Getaway

• Book 5 •
Crafting an Alibi

• Book 6 •
Crafting a Cold Case

DEDICATION

For Poppy and Rhea, who understand chickens and so much else.

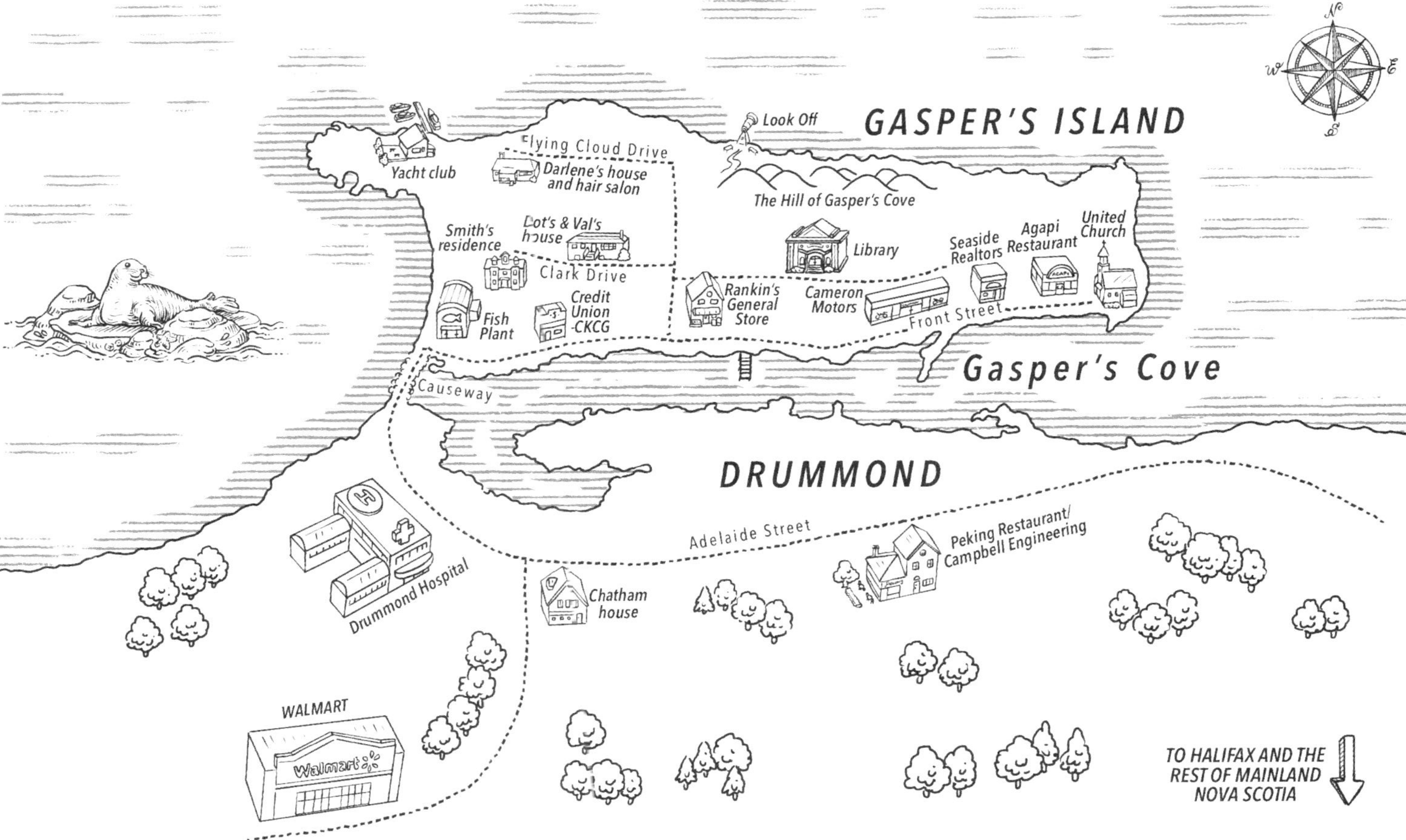
GASPER'S ISLAND
Look Off
Yacht club
Flying Cloud Drive
Darlene's house and hair salon
The Hill of Gasper's Cove
Smith's residence
Dot's & Val's house
Clark Drive
Library
Seaside Realtors
Agapi Restaurant
United Church
Fish Plant
Credit Union -CKCG
Rankin's General Store
Cameron Motors
Front Street
Gasper's Cove
Causeway
DRUMMOND
Adelaide Street
Peking Restaurant/ Campbell Engineering
Drummond Hospital
Chatham house
WALMART
Walmart
TO HALIFAX AND THE REST OF MAINLAND NOVA SCOTIA

CHAPTER ONE

I picked up the brand-new ball of sock wool. I settled into my chair. I'd walked the dog, talked to my store, texted the family, done the breakfast dishes, and put in a wash. I had saved this yarn, bright pink and turquoise, for a gray day.

It was February. Christmas was over. The spring birthdays were months away.

This pair was for me.

I picked up my needles to cast on.

Next to my cup of tea on the side table, my phone beeped. I put down my needles and looked at the screen.

Emergency. Get here ASAP before I kill somebody.

What?

I tapped back.

Catherine Walker, ex-librarian and bed-and-breakfast commander-in-chief, never lost her cool. She was as good at that as I wasn't. I knew in my heart that if terrorists ever kidnapped me and locked me up in outer Siberia, it would be Catherine who would find me and set me free. Of course, that would come with a talking-to about my reckless behavior, but I knew she wouldn't leave me unsaved.

That something had rattled her scared me.

What's going on?

I tried again.

Tell me.

I added.

No response. ASAP. That meant now.

On my way.

I pressed end and jumped out of my chair. I threw my wool and needles into my knitting basket, ran over to the hall closet, and pulled out my insulated winter coat, fair isle tuque, and thrummed wool mittens. Toby, my golden retriever, watched me dress. I didn't usually move this fast.

"Don't worry," I reassured him. "I'll be back soon. Everything is fine."

Toby sighed and lay down. He didn't believe me. I didn't blame him.

I closed the front door behind me. Behind it, I heard Toby run over to the couch to watch me leave from the bungalow's picture window. I grabbed the railing and stepped down. I'd put salt on the steps, and I was glad of it now. They were ice-free, unlike the path to the driveway, or what I could see of the street. There had been some melting during the day, but at 4:30 in the afternoon, the sun was beginning its slow exit.

Not long until it would freeze and be slippery again. I'd be careful driving on the Shore Road.

I sat in the driveway before I left, running the car to let the engine warm up. There was still no message back from Catherine. I turned up the heater and tuned in to the local station, CKGC.

... and now for the weather. The current wave of arctic air is lifting folks, with temperatures to climb near to above freezing over the next few days, starting in the morning. Until then, don't forget to dress up and make sure those pets are not left outside too long. As always, frostbite and hypothermia can happen this time of year. But that's February in Nova Scotia, and we're used to it.

This was not news. I turned the radio off and backed out of my driveway. What was Catherine's emergency?

When I arrived at the Inn Catherine co-owned with my cousin Rollie, everything looked normal from the outside. The old sea captain's homestead, a massive dark-red Victorian three-story structure, windows and doors defined by elaborate woodwork skillfully carved by the same craftsmen who had built schooners, stood on three acres above the North Atlantic. The take-your-breath-away view was beautiful in the summer, but now the winter sea under the cliffs at the end of the property was wild and gray. The fair-weather months, May to late October, were when the bed-and-breakfast did most of its business. Guests this time of year were infrequent. As far as I knew, the only occupants of the Inn this month were Rollie, Catherine, and the Inn's overweight, much-indulged, gray cat, Dusty. Catherine had no problem keeping Rollie and Dusty in line, so if she was on the verge of murder, someone else was involved. I wondered who they were.

I pushed the Inn's heavy oak door open and stepped into the entry to find out. I took off my coat, pushed my mitts and hat down into a sleeve, and hung it up on one of the hooks on the faded, cabbage-rose wallpaper to the right of the door. The reception desk was empty.

"Catherine?" I walked down the long, high-ceilinged hall to find her, past the pictures of the stern, mono-tinted faces of the community's past schooner captains, successful boat builders, pirates, rumrunners and a few politicians. That last group was out of place, memorable as they were, for ambition, not skill or nerve.

"It's me, Valerie," I called again. "I got here as fast as I could."

No answer.

This didn't feel right, not right at all.

I heard a noise. Banging at the end of the hall. Metal on metal. Angry sounds from behind a closed door. I ran down and opened the door to the kitchen.

Inside, the Bluenose Inn's front-desk manager was on the floor, surrounded by cookware.

"Catherine? What's going on? What's the emergency? Why the pots?" I noticed the reference-desk librarian turned innkeeper had a measuring tape in one of her hands, a pencil behind her ear, and what looked like a detailed map, or battlefield diagram, in her lap.

My friend and my cousin's love interest glanced up at me. She looked like she wanted to cry. This horrified me. I had never seen tears in Catherine's eyes before. She wasn't the type. Losing composure was my job, not hers.

Catherine didn't answer. Instead, she pulled a twisted tissue from the sleeve of the cotton turtleneck she wore under her quilted vest and blew her nose loudly, like an old man. The noise startled me. Catherine was an accomplished quilter, the kind who felt the more pieces the better, with a competitive twelve hand stitches per inch. Self-control was her middle name, but now she was too upset to speak. Instead, she held up a paper for me to read. I took it from her damp hand and sat down on a kitchen chair. There were no words, only a diagram of shelves, the dimensions carefully marked with double-headed arrows. I stared at Catherine. It looked to me as though the crumpled woman on the floor was measuring her cookware and plotting its placement on the shelves. I was shocked. If locked in a kitchen with a tape measure for a hundred million years, I'd never think to do this.

"Is this your crisis?" It was my turn to be at a loss for words. "The pots?"

Catherine grabbed the edge of a counter and pulled herself to her feet. "No. I just find organizing is the only thing that calms me down when I'm losing it. Like when I have trouble sleeping, I lie in bed at night and arrange things in my mind. Do you ever do that?"

"Never," I answered truthfully. I tried again. "What's got you so upset?"

"The prepper," she said. "He's down in the basement with Rollie right now, in the dark, with the pipes. Every time we turn around, he is watching us. He says he's preparing for the end of time. Here. In my bed-and-breakfast." She pressed her forehead against a kitchen cupboard and sniffed. I'd never seen Catherine this distressed. Not even the time she arrived at a quilting get-together without her quarter-inch foot.

"You have to tell me more," I said. "Who are you talking about?"

"Someone I brought here. It's all my fault. He'll never leave, I can feel it." Catherine dragged herself over to a chair and collapsed. "He'll be here forever, waiting for disaster," she said. "Unless I can find a way to make him disappear."

I knew what to do.

CHAPTER TWO

I went over to the pantry and found the box of Morse's Tea, the official consolation beverage of Nova Scotia since 1870. I picked up the kettle and filled it at the deep, stainless-steel, industrial-size sink. While I waited for the water to boil, I found a tin of shortbread and put enough for four people onto a plate. Emotional breakdowns are no time to be skimpy with baked goods.

I poured the tea and put one cup in front of Catherine and sat down. "Why don't you start from the beginning and tell me what this is about," I heard myself say in my visitor-to-the-hospital voice. Catherine was not herself. It was required.

The measuring tape was still in Catherine's hands. She wound and unwound it as we talked.

"You know I miss the library, don't you?" she asked.

I considered the call numbers on the alphabetized books in the Inn's tiny guest library. "I do," I said.

"When I retired to come here with Rollie—not that I regret that for one minute—it meant that we spent every minute of every day together. Not that I don't love that. But being the center of the action in a public library ... it's not something you get over." The slightly damp tissue reappeared from Catherine's sleeve. "I miss the excitement," she sniffed.

"I can see that," I said even though I couldn't, not completely.

"I'm on the Board," Catherine said. The statement perked her up. "Policy always was my strength. In fact, I was the one who proposed the visiting-author program. I admit that."

We each took a shortbread. Rollie must have baked them. If he hadn't trained as a psychologist, he could have been a chef.

"Nothing wrong with that as an idea," I said. "Lots of artists and writers come here. Professors on sabbatical too. We're good with those kinds of people."

"You think?" Catherine snorted. "Wait 'til we get to Part 2 of it all going to hell in a handbasket with my proposal. I mean, I meant well. I'll say that in my own defense. I had this idea to bring in published authors, give them a place to stay—in our case, here at the Inn—and time to write, for a small stipend. In return, they could run some programs at the library." She struggled with the next words, as if it mortified her to say them. "Rollie gets restless over the quiet months." Catherine dabbed her nose again. "I thought if I could get a writer, an intellectual, here over the winter, Rollie would have some distraction. And that would take the pressure off me so I could do my own projects." She looked wistfully at the pot-shelf diagram.

"Sounds like a great idea," I offered.

Catherine picked up her tea and took a sip. "Thanks. But I needed a way to sell my plan to the library, something from the programming point of view that would make a writer-in-residence make sense. Then, I had a brainwave to find an author who worked in young adult fiction. That way, we could get our teenagers involved—you know, a writing group, maybe some readings, in-house publication."

"Smart," I said. "That's a hard group to keep busy."

"I did my research," Catherine continued. "I presented the Board with a shortlist of YA authors to contact. I looked for fantasy types, since that's all kids read since *Harry Potter.*" Catherine added two spoons of sugar to her tea. She didn't usually take sugar. "That's when I came up with Simon Broadbent." She noted the blank look on my face. "You know the *Magik Markers* series? It's famous."

"Haven't read it, but I'll take your word for it."

"Simon accepted, moved in here last week, and started at the library," Catherine said.

"And the problem is ...," I coaxed.

"He's changed genres and didn't tell us. He decided to give up fiction and switch to nonfiction. Self-help." Catherine's voice was shaky.

"Helping anyone, even yourself, is a good thing," I suggested.

"No, you don't understand." She glared at me. "Simon is a *prepper.* The main reason he wanted to come here to Gasper's Cove, a little island off the coast, was because he thought we could teach him about life in extreme adversity. He wants to write a book about it. We are his research." She rolled her eyes. I thought indignation looked better on her than tears. "As a result, since he arrived, he has stalked us while we do sensible things, like cutting wood, putting on snow tires, adding antifreeze to the car, buying seeds for the bird feeder—all the usual stuff anyone does. And if we make eye contact with him, out comes his phone, and he starts recording. He's slowing us down. Rollie has jobs to do." Catherine picked up a shortbread and snapped it in two. "But where has he been the last two hours? Down in the basement with Doomsday Simon, stuck to him like glue, explaining what happens if pipes freeze in the winter."

Who didn't already know about the pipes? They had to be insulated, and the supply to the outside turned off. Water expanded when it got below freezing. Burst pipes were an awful mess. "How long is this writer-in-resident thing?" I asked. "When does this Simon guy go?"

"In *six months*," Catherine said. "He wants to stay until the book is done."

I'd waited out odd houseguests before myself. It wasn't easy. "Oh boy. I can see your problem. What's the book called anyway?"

"*A Beginning Survivalist's Guide to the Coming Apocalypse*," Catherine said. "Although I am pretty sure that the one who's not going to survive is me."

I went to the counter and plugged the kettle back in. This was clearly a two-pot problem.

When I returned to the table, all the shortbread was gone.

"Alright," I said. Someone had to take charge. "First thing to do is to tell Rollie not to let this prepper person use up all his time." I looked around the large kitchen, with its brand-new dishwasher and six-burner stove. "This is a big place. It needs two people full-time to run it."

"I tried that. It didn't work," Catherine said. "You know Rollie, he's a teacher at heart. I think a big part of him likes explaining things all day. It's my own fault Simon is here. I can't get Rollie's attention anyway. Which brings us to problem number two."

"What else is going on?" I got up and filled the plate with more shortbread.

"Not a what, a who," Catherine corrected. "It turns out that I wasn't the only one who figured Rollie needed some stimulation to get through the winter. He had the same idea himself. So, *without talking to me*"—Catherine's spoon stabbed the sugar bowl—"he invited an old prof friend of his to come and stay. The man arrived two days after Simon. His name's Gareth Davies. He taught archeology. Rollie took classes with him before he switched over to psychology. Gareth's interest is in northern exploration—Iceland, Greenland, Newfoundland, places like that. If you see him, put your head down. Keep walking if you want to get anything done that day. Even hint at anything historical, and he'll corner you with a fourteen-hour lecture. Apparently, Gareth was here in the middle of his career. He worked for a summer between university appointments for some Scandinavian archeologist no one knows much about. Gareth hadn't been here since, but he claims being here is completing this intellectual cycle."

This sounded suspicious to me. Winter in Gasper's Cove was better known as an ideal place for catching up on knitting, quilting, and making granny-square blankets than as an academic destination. But I felt Catherine needed some positivity. "At least he sounds interesting," I suggested.

Catherine snorted. "Rollie thinks so. Simon loves him too. You should hear the conversation at the dinner table. More talk about sealskins than anyone needs to hear." Catherine sighed. "And he smokes. A pipe. Who does that these days? I caught Rollie cleaning out an old pipe of his dad's from a drawer. I can't have that."

"Back to the emergency," I said. "I can see how all this is stressful. I understand why these two situations are hard, but if you don't mind me asking, why did you text me? What do you want me to do?"

"Look," Catherine said, putting her spoon down on her plate. I could see she was ready to get down to business. "This is the situation. It's the end of February. In Nova Scotia. We're all stuck inside. I'm living with three men, and only one of them I like. You'd think that a writer and old professor would give Rollie something to think about and settle him down. I'm afraid the opposite is happening. I'm afraid it's reminding Rollie of the big world of ideas that he's missing living here, in this life, with me. I need the prepper and the professor to find somewhere else to stay or at least some other place to go during the days so Rollie and I can get back to being a unit."

So, that was her scheme.

"You're not suggesting one of these characters stay with me, are you?" I asked. "Look, I have a daughter here who came all the way from Scotland to be a bridesmaid when Darlene got married. I'm going to have her here for another couple of weeks. Plus, Kay's got a friend coming. I'm busy."

Catherine narrowed her eyes. "Kay isn't staying with you, is she? She's over at Darlene's, taking care of the cats while the happy couple is off on their honeymoon. Am I right?"

She had me there. My cousin Darlene had finally married George Kosoulos, twenty-five years after they had first gone steady in high school. They were in Cuba, having an all-inclusive honeymoon, whatever that was. Kay, writing her dissertation for a graduate program in veterinary medicine, had been her first and best choice as house sitter.

"I don't care, Catherine. I'm not going to have strange men staying with me at my house." There were never men of any kind at my house, but that was beside the point. "But I will help get them out of your hair."

For the first time since I'd arrived, Catherine smiled. I realized she already had everything worked out, and our conversation up to this point had just been part of her lure.

She reeled me in.

"Thank you," she said. "Here's my idea for Gareth. There's a group that meets out of"—she paused to gather her strength before she, the owner of a classy bed-and-breakfast, could say the name of her lower-standards rival—"the Anchor Motel in Drummond. They call themselves the Treasure Trovers. Old guys with metal detectors on the beaches, grown-up boys cracking beach rocks open, looking for fossils. They used to make us crazy at the library. They'd bring chips of road asphalt they claimed were volcanic rock, green pennies they found flattened on railway tracks they thought were pirate treasure. The Anchor's got a display for the tourists. They'd be delighted to have a real archeologist like Gareth speak to them."

"You want your guest to visit the Anchor? Are you sure?" I asked. The Bluenose Inn, with its higher level of accommodations, had cut into the business once done by the casually renovated motel across the causeway. At one point, Danny Dwyer, the manager of the Anchor, had even gone so far in retaliation as to suggest the Inn had bedbugs, a problem he knew well. One public health visit later, which had turned up nothing, he apologized for spreading false information, but he and Catherine had avoided each other since. But I remembered Catherine was as meticulous in revenge as she was in organizing. Sending Rollie's old professor across the causeway would get him out of her hair and irritate a competitor.

"But how do I fit into this?"

Catherine's smile was broad but crafty. "Gareth doesn't drive. He must be at least eighty. He lost his license. His eyesight is going." She let this sink in. "You know Rollie and I can't take him over and see Danny. Could you do it? As a favor? For us? The group meets every other Wednesday at 6:00. This is one of their weeks. What do you say?"

I tried to think of an excuse but couldn't come up with one fast enough.

"Okay," I said.

"Excellent," Catherine said, ushering me out of the kitchen and into the hall. "That brings us to Simon."

"The prepper? Let me guess: You want me to chauffeur him to some survivalist gathering you've located."

"No, not at all," Catherine's smile was stiff. "That one's writing a book on self-sufficiency. Loner stuff. But guess what he wants to do?"

"No idea."

"Sew," Catherine said, unrolling her punchline with a flourish. "And I told him you'd love to teach him."

CHAPTER THREE

I opened my mouth to tell Catherine that this was a dumb idea when Rollie and a thin, young man in his early thirties surfaced from the basement. I studied the newcomer in his faded black turtleneck and black corduroy pants, the wales worn at the knees. The pants, hitched up high and gathered like jodhpurs over his bony hips, looked like hand-me-downs from an older, larger brother.

Someone like Rollie.

I understood Catherine's problem.

My cousin Rollie's face was flushed with enthusiasm and authority above his red beard. Having a student, a fan, clearly agreed with him. Looking around for another lesson prop, he stooped down and picked up a draft stopper, one of the many I had made for the Inn's aging and ill-fitting doors, and presented it to the visitor, who took it reverently, like a gift.

"One of the issues in an old house like this," Rollie explained, "as tight as it was when the shipbuilders made it, is that over time, the wood has dried out and shrunk.

That's why you see these gaps outside between the shingles and inside between these oak boards." Rollie tapped the floor with his shoe and waited until the visitor, presumably Simon Broadbent, bent down and took several close-up shots with his phone's camera. "The winter wind has a way of coming inside and finding you." Rollie paused, clearly enjoying an opportunity to exhibit his flair for description.

Simon gingerly stroked the plaid flannel draft stopper, a sewn sausage, door width and four inches high, with his long white fingers. He raised his phone to his mouth and dictated:

"A traditional device designed to protect the inhabitants of shelters from the intrusion of the outside elements, made by hand and pushed under the bottom of doors to seal out the cold and seal in the warmth." He raised his eyebrows up above the rim of his heavy-framed black glasses, as if wanting Rollie to confirm this was an accurate interpretation. When Rollie nodded, he continued. "These units are remarkably heavy. No doubt filled with found materials—sand from the coastline, or possibly sawdust from hardwood in the old-growth forest, manually harvested, of course."

I'd had enough.

"I made these draft stoppers," I said. "I filled them with kitty litter. From the Foodmart."

I wasn't sure, but I thought I saw a flash of annoyance on the survivalist's face. I wasn't the only one annoyed.

A smooth, narrow hand extended. "And you are?" he asked.

"Valerie Rankin, manager of Rankin's General Store and the Crafter's Co-op." Catherine nudged me from behind. "Also, local sewing teacher." Catherine gently body checked my shoulder with hers. "You must be Simon. I understand you want to learn how to sew. I run a couple of classes." Another bump from behind. "We'd love to have you." To make the point, I took Simon's hand and shook it. It felt slim, damp, and limp in my hand, like a caught mackerel.

There was a shift in Simon's attitude, as he reclassified me from a kitty litter–purchasing philistine into someone useful.

"That would be perfect," he said crisply. "I know exactly what I want to make. I have some hand-loomed wool I brought from a trip to the Hebrides and some yarn dyed with lichen from a local man. I am thinking of wool trousers with a button fly as well as a lined winter jacket. I've done my research. When they're done, I thought I would pick up some knitting skills and make myself a couple of Guernsey sweaters from heritage patterns. Oh, I almost forgot, once I source a trapper and tanner, whip up some boots and some shoes. Keep it to the basics to start. But first, the easy stuff, like sewing. More entry-level skills."

My cousin Rollie had the sense to back away. "I think," he said, "it's time I fed the cat."

I ignored him.

"That's quite the agenda," I said to Simon. "How much time do you have?"

"Free three days a week and weekends," Simon said. "I'll be here for the winter. A couple of months. How long are your sessions?"

"Depends on which ones," I said. "How much sewing experience do you have?"

"Oh, lots," Simon said. "Many on the conceptual level, as someone who has worn clothing their whole life. Oh, and

I once watched an elderly woman hem pants. And then there's my education. In Home Ec in grade ten, we made pillowcases. Got a B+," he said. "I deserved an A. Something about right sides together."

Years ago, when he was still a psychologist, Rollie had taught me how to breathe. I did that now: one breath in, one long, slow breath out. I looked again at Simon's loose pants, gathered by a leather belt at his waist so they flowed like a shirt over his hips. The man's fitting standards were low. He had no idea what he didn't know.

I did a mental scan of my upcoming classes, skipping over Wednesday evenings, now committed to archeologist transport.

"Six o'clock. *Tailoring for the Terrified. Drop-in UFOs* on Saturday afternoons. How does that sound?" I asked.

"UFOs?" Simon was offended. "Tailoring, yes, space aliens, no. I no longer write fantasy."

This man didn't know what a UFO was. I'd have to start at the beginning. "Unfinished objects. Projects that aren't done. It's a nice group. They come in and try to help each other get through. Skirts without hems, quilts without binding. Things like that."

"Ahh. A gathering of local artisans." The light went on in Simon's eyes. "An ideal environment for gathering more information on generational knowledge. It shouldn't take me long to make what I want. Then, we can talk. Count me in."

I wondered if the crafters would ever forgive me.

I woke up the next morning to a beep on my bedside table. Toby stirred beside me and rolled over onto his back. I reached over and turned on a light and picked up my phone.

A message from Darlene.

What's the news?

I sat up, put a pillow behind my back, and tried to think of what to tell her.

All good here. Catherine's got some weird guests. A guy writing a prepper book and an old prof of Rollie's. How's Cuba?

Hot. Nice. Guess who we met?

Who?

Duck. He's staying here too. How weird is that?

Weird.

I answered.

The store's handyman, Duck Macdonald, had taken a week off to go "somewhere sunny." I knew his options were limited. Once incarcerated because of the counterfeiting scheme his nitwit brothers had gotten him tangled up in, Duck could only cross borders where not too many questions were asked about criminal records. It made sense he was in Cuba. I hoped he remembered Darlene and George were on their honeymoon.

Nice to have someone we know here.

Three bubbles bounced on my phone—Darlene had more to say.

Miss you ❤

Have fun.

I tapped back.

See you soon.

I was fully awake now. The mention of Duck reminded me that Shadow, Rankin's General Store's resident cat, would be waiting for her breakfast. She normally went home with Duck on the weekends but spent weekdays in the store. On those days, Duck fed her.

My day had started. I pushed Toby over, swung my feet to the floor, and headed down the hall to the kitchen to make coffee.

It was still dark when Toby and I drove down the hill. The temperature was still well below freezing, and the water on the wharf side of Front Street was as dark as the sky, but deeper, almost menacing. The radio assured me that the day would be mild, verified by information from the station's weather station, a shed with meteorological equipment on the hill near the look-off. Like the rest of the community, I found these reports more reliable than those that came from satellites and the computers in the nation's capital. As CKGC liked to say, all news was local, and so was the weather.

Arriving at the store always gave me a lift. The business had been in my family for more than a century, and it was now my turn to manage. For generations, we had been the only store in town selling fishing supplies, tools, and whatever else a small island needed to survive. Thirty years ago, that had changed. A causeway over the water, connecting tiny Gasper's Cove with the town of Drummond on the mainland, had been built. Suddenly, the modern world, with all its products and conveniences, was only a short drive away.

In the years that followed the construction of the causeway, it had seemed inevitable that Rankin's General would close, as so many small family-owned stores across the province had. The tourists saved us. As it turned out, what we had traditionally done while the rest of the world had passed us by was exactly what they were looking for. To them, everything we'd done to make do was the work of artisans, even art. These summer visitors saw value in the quilts, carving, pottery, knitting, woodwork, and weaving we made and stockpiled over the long, isolated winters, and they enjoyed chatting with the people who had made them.

And so the Crafter's Co-op was born. We'd turned the second floor of the store into a consignment shop run by volunteers, and Rankin's General was rescued by the craftiness of a skilled community, always able, when required, to make something out of nothing.

I wondered who would watch over the store after me. My older son had joined the Royal Canadian Mounted Police and was off training. My younger son was a vegan baker in Brooklyn. My daughter, Kay, was too educated to be a shopkeeper. I knew the dissertation she was writing over at Darlene's house, surrounded by cats, was the last step in her program. I wanted to know what her plans were for after she graduated, but I didn't know when and how to ask.

Daughters, unlike sons, could hear the real question behind your words, like "Are you ever coming home?"

The main thing was that she was now here in Gasper's Cove. I stamped my feet on the mat. I was surprised to see Kay was at the store, talking to my aunt and front-counter assistant Colleen. Tall, slim, and beautiful, Kay was more poised and composed than I had been at that age, or was now.

"Hey, Mom," she said when she saw me. "Lucky I'm here. There's someone I want you to meet. A friend in from Scotland."

Behind her, Colleen widened her eyes, as if trying to telegraph some important information to me without speaking. I gave her a tiny shrug.

Kay missed all this; she wasn't listening to me. Her full attention was on a young man strolling toward us from one of the aisles, laced shoes scuffed but very expensive, hands in his jeans pockets, the edges of his button-down shirt tucked down inside the crew neckline of his cashmere sweater.

The charisma crossed the room and hit me. He was tall and thin, with a face shaved sometime last week, thick, curly red-brown hair brushed the week before that, and the kind of nose that runs in the family. He was not, by ordinary standards, good-looking. Some people don't have to be. I understood the look on Colleen's face: It was awe.

Before I could recover, this amazing young man stepped forward, grabbed my shoulders, and pulled me into a hug. He smelled like nutmeg. I wondered if he cooked. Close to him, my intuition murmured.

"Mrs. Rankin? Can I call you Valerie? I have *so* been looking forward to meeting you." Over the high, thin shoulder hard under my chin, I saw Colleen beam and my daughter smile.

"I'm Tristan."

He let go. I stepped back. I was aware of my boots, my parka, and the wool hat on my head. "Tristan," I repeated. He was the first Tristan I'd ever met. "I've heard so much about you." This wasn't true. Was this a friend, or a boyfriend? I had no idea. "How long are you here?" I couldn't think of anything else to say.

"Only a week or so. Busy. Big story. I'm sorry I missed the wedding. I hear you danced all night." This Tristan had a lovely Transatlantic accent. I wondered if he was a North American who lived in the United Kingdom or an Englishman who had lived over here.

"True enough. You missed quite a time. Kay's aunt married George Kosoulos—his family owns the Agapi restaurant in town. Big Greek wedding; they sure know how to dance," I rambled.

Tristan laughed. "I won't make that mistake again. It sounds like great material."

Material? Were we talking about sewing? I raised my eyebrows at my daughter. "Tristan is an independent broadcaster," she explained. Her eyes telegraphed for me to not ask too many questions.

"What's that?" Colleen asked. "Sounds important."

Tristan's beautifully matted curls fell over one eye. He flicked them away with a practiced shake of his head.

"I'm not important at all, but my subjects are. That's why I do what I do," he said.

Kay rushed in to elaborate. "Tristan has a true-crime podcast. He talks about unsolved crimes, you know, cold cases. Murders where the killer was never caught."

I didn't know what to say. And how often did that happen to me? In the silence, I did a quick assessment. A podcaster? I wondered if that was a position with a pension plan or benefits. Probably not. I was also pretty sure it wasn't a union job.

"How did you get into that?" I asked. "Take a course?"

Kay laughed loudly, to convey to her friend that her mother had a terrific sense of humor and often said witty things like this.

"No," Tristan said, giving me his full attention, like there was no one else in the room. I could see what Kay saw in him. "I grew up in a town where a man on our street was murdered. They never found out who killed him. But everyone had a theory. I saw firsthand what it did to otherwise-decent people when they suspected each other. It's like a poison that can infect a community. I guess I became obsessed with telling the stories of these unsolved crimes."

"And he's very good at it," Kay interjected. "True crime is the most listened-to subject in podcasting, with an audience of millions. He's looking for sponsorship money."

"Wow," Colleen said. "Good for you. I'll have to get one of the grandchildren to show me how to do podcasts. What's your show called?"

"*Solved and Resolved*," our impressive visitor said. "I know it sounds dramatic, but I try to find a little peace for people. No one can heal and move on if they never know what happened. I do what I can. I hope it helps."

CHAPTER FOUR

After Kay and Tristan left, I went into my office, shut the door, and texted Darlene.

Met Kay's friend.

What's he like?

Good manners.

That's not telling me what you think of him. Would I like him?

I hesitated. It was always hard to know what Darlene would think.

I am sure you would. Your mom loves him.

😂 That means he's got a good head of hair. Her weakness.

How's married life?

I was ready to change the subject.

Worth waiting for. Got to go. Duck and George have ordered mojitos.

Enjoy. Miss you. ❤

I sighed and put my phone away. I hated texting. Enough words to get you into trouble, not enough to say what you meant.

I spent the rest of the day working, downstairs selling plastic film to householders sealing up old windows, and upstairs in the Co-op, setting out a display of new mitts. Once or twice, I thought I heard rustling at the back of the shelves, noises in the basement. Shadow, I decided, must be doing what store cats do best: dealing with any small rodents that had snuck in away from the cold. The time passed quickly, and before I knew it, it was time for me to go and remove one Professor Emeritus from the Bluenose Inn and deposit him at the Anchor Motel.

When I arrived at the Inn, Gareth was waiting for me, standing outside the front door on the porch like a cat that wanted to come in.

I hurried out of the truck I had borrowed from the store and helped him down the stairs.

"Hello, Gareth, and how are you this evening?" I asked, sounding more like an Uber driver than myself, which, given the circumstances, was not surprising.

"Splendid." The retired archeologist handed me his cane, and I helped him step up into the truck. It was awkward to drive, but good in the snow. It also had a cab on the back for deliveries and heated seats, something my old car did not. Even with this luxury, it did not look like Gareth enjoyed the truck. His mouth tightened under his white goatee, and he pulled the navy tam on his head lower, adjusted the worn Black Watch scarf around his neck, loosened the seatbelt over the straining buttons of his tweed coat, and pronounced, "I am ready."

I gave him back his cane.

"Thank you," he said, placing it between his knees and regaining his composure. "A little extra security when I walk on the ice. Do you know that in Inuktitut, the language of the Canadian Inuit, there are, with regional derivations, at least ninety-three words for snow and ice?"

I did not know that. "My mom used to call a little bit of snowfall a skiff," I offered over my shoulder, backing out onto the main road into town.

I didn't think Gareth heard me.

"In Nunavik, there are at least that many words for sea ice alone," he continued, raising his voice to drown out possible contributions from me. "*Qautsaulittuq* is ice that breaks under a harpoon."

I turned up the heater to High.

"*Iniruvik* is ice that has thawed and refrozen," Gareth continued.

The snow in front of my lights changed to flurries. The wind had picked up, blurring the headlights of oncoming vehicles. I turned on the wipers and punched the defrost button on the dashboard. The steam of conversation inside the car fogged the inside of the windshield. I used my mitt to clear a space so I could see. I bent down low to peer through the band of visibility melted by the heater.

"And *Illusaq* is snow packed hard enough to make an igloo ..."

The truck skidded, and I looked ahead to the causeway. It would be salted and ice-free. We were almost there.

"Did Catherine tell you about this group you're going to meet?" I asked, more loudly than intended, cutting my passenger off in mid-dissertation. "The Treasure Trovers?"

Gareth seemed disorientated by the shift in topic but rallied. "I expect there will be quite the turnout when the word gets out I am attending. It means a lot to an amateur to meet an expert. As a public service throughout my career, I always made time for public speaking. So often, these groups have no concept of excavation protocols or the principles of rigorous documentation. And most of the time, what they find is of no consequence, but occasionally ..."

I turned on CKGC and drove.

Across the causeway, I saw the flashing sign of the Anchor Motel not a quarter of a mile away. Next to me, Gareth listed every public gathering he had attended in the last three decades, chuckling at how witty he'd been at each one.

I listened silently—there was no other choice—and looked for the best place to offload my passenger. I saw that the "r" and "M" had burned out on the Anchor's sign. The pulsing neon now read "Ancho otel" and was framed on either side with two giant, exhaust-dirty piles of solid snow, each at least a dozen feet high, standing on either side of the front entrance like sentries. I maneuvered my way between them, stopping under the canopy of the front entrance, leaving the truck running as I struggled around rutted ice to open Gareth's door. I felt like some middle-aged, slightly reluctant, sewing-teacher version of a parking valet.

"Here we are," I said. "Right on time for your meeting."

"Do you know the difference between the words *motel* and *hotel*?" Gareth asked as he rocked himself back and forth to gain momentum to lift himself out of the passenger seat.

"Nope."

"A hotel has historically provided accommodations and meals." He was up and out, his slip-on rubber overshoes, just big enough to cover the soles of his leather Oxfords, sinking into the snow when he stepped down. "Whereby a motel offers only accommodations and parking. A mid-20th-century phenomenon ..." Briefly, Gareth noticed his environment and eyed the incomplete Anchor sign. "... Of which this appears to be an unaltered example."

Before the professor could enlighten me further, the twin front doors of the motel opened, and two men came out. One was the Anchor's manager, Danny Dwyer, and the other I recognized as Percy Skinner, the Trovers' leader, a metal-detecting regular on Gasper's beach, and the creator of pirate maps he sold to trusting tourists. Neither man had a winter jacket or boots on. They waited for us close to the door, stamping their feet on the salted outdoor mat.

Danny was the first to come forward and grab Gareth's hand. "An honor, sir," he said, using his practiced meeting-with-the-president-of-the-Rotary hospitality manager voice. "An expert in the field, come to our community, drawn, I'm sure, by the richness of our history."

Percy angled his shoulder to move Danny out of the way. "Likewise," he said. "As the president of the Gasper's Cove and Greater Drummond Treasure Trovers, I'd like to welcome you. It will be good to have a colleague in the area. I always welcome a second opinion."

Gareth seemed taken aback. For an awkward moment, he hesitated before he let go of Danny's hand and took Percy's. I avoided all eyes and instead studied the iron boot scraper outside the motel's door to hide my smile. Colleague? Had Percy forgotten local ears could hear him? Ones that knew he left school after grade eight, having completed most of his education in the principal's office?

"Ah, charmed," Gareth said formally. "Delighted to address your group." He pulled off his wool scarf and tam with a flourish, lifted his cane, and strode forward, fully committed to his archeological public information mission. "Did you know," he asked Percy, "that the origins of the phrase *treasure trove* came from the French? *Tresor trové*, possibly adopted by the English in the late 12th century?"

"I knew that," Percy said, running a finger under the neck of his shirt.

"Then you know that the French borrowed the term from the Latin, *thesaurus inventus*, something valuable that was saved, possibly also incorporating the past participle of *trover*, the French verb 'to find'"—Gareth had shifted into rhetorical cruise control—"itself developed from the Latin *turbare*, translated by some scholars as 'to disturb' ..."

"You don't say," Percy interrupted, nudging the visitor down a narrow hall to the right of the motel's reception desk. "The meeting room's this way. Wait 'til you see what we've got laid out to show you. An old plumb bob, maybe 18th-century, buddy found in his backyard when he was moving the rhubarb; coins we retrieved from the wishing well at Oceanview Park, working on dating those; some broken dishes they dug up at a building site, figured they were left behind by a family in the Great Upheaval, you know, when the British kicked the Acadians out of Nova Scotia. And my find, the big one, a photograph of a stone, I need to send it on for that carbon-dating stuff. Not sure how we'll get it down to Halifax to the lab at the university. And they'd probably charge us to do it. Might have to have a bake sale. ..."

Gareth ignored him and started to make his way to a sign that said "GC and GD Treasure Trovers. New Members Welcome" on an easel beside an open door. I felt his unease. No doubt running into someone with as many words as he had was a new experience.

"We'll see," he said, "I will give you my assessment of your collection." His voice trailed away as he and Danny disappeared through the open door. "Happy to lend my expertise to distinguish the authentic and significant from the incidental and unimportant."

I wished the Treasure Trovers luck.

Percy went to follow them, then stopped. "Valerie, I meant it. You know, about a fundraiser for lab work on my discovery? I thought maybe set up a table or pledge sheet some morning at the store? What do you think?"

I hesitated. Rankin's General liked to support local initiatives; I wondered if carbon dating fell into that category. I felt Percy watching me, a small man in a coat that looked too big for him, an enthusiast propelled through life by the intensity of his interests. He and I had that in common.

"Sure," I said, wondering if I would later regret it. "We can work something out."

I'd never seen Percy smile before. "We got a deal then," he said. "Tell you what. You give me a hand with this, and I'll let you in on a little secret. Not now"—he looked around—"but later. I know you'll keep it to yourself. I wouldn't say this to many in this town, but I trust you. Your people have always been reliable."

I didn't know what to say to this, but that didn't matter. Before Percy could say anything more, Danny stuck his head out of the door to the meeting room.

"Percy," he called out. "Get in here. They're waiting for you."

"Coming!" Percy turned to me and then shook my hand, sealing a deal he felt we had made, his knuckles gnarled with arthritis, but his grip tight. He then turned and walked into the room, passing the motel manager on the way out.

The door closed.

Danny came to stand beside me. "What's about to happen tonight in that room, my dear, is the launching of the next part of a grand, probably brilliant, scheme to put Drummond and Gasper's Cove on the map."

I stared at the motel manager. "A plan? To do what?"

"Attract global tourism, the big bucks." Danny slapped his hands together and rubbed them, overcome with the excitement of his highly prosperous future.

"Am I missing something?" I asked. "What you have here is a bunch of nice, harmless old guys bringing in stuff they found on their dog walks and a retired professor who won't stop talking. How is *that* going to draw crowds?"

"The United Nations," Danny answered. "You got to think big, my girl. When news of the archeological significance of this community gets out, they'll be lining up. If Lunenburg and Newfoundland can do it, we can."

"Do what?"

"Get this area designated a World Heritage Site," Danny said. "The outfit that does it is UNESCO, the United Nations Educational, Scientific and Cultural Organization. L'Anse aux Meadows got it up there at the rear end of Newfoundland because they found a Norse settlement from the 11th century. Ever been there?"

I shook my head.

"Place is a big deal with the European folks—no limit to what that crowd will pay for accommodations. It's just rocks and the Newfoundland weather, mind you, but they're tourists, am I right? They don't care. And Lunenburg? Not that far down the coast from here, the size of Gasper's Cove. Now they've got Hollywood people filming there every week because it's so picturesque. And you know why? The place looks like it did 300 years ago. That's all. No progress. And they're raking it in because of it." Danny narrowed his eyes as if wondering whether I was sharp enough to catch the implications of what he said. "You see where I am going with this?" he asked.

"Maybe? Not sure. Why don't you tell me?" I suggested.

"Think about it. We got rocks, we got bad weather, especially in the winter. Every building we got here in downtown Drummond and every little part of Gasper's Cove is old. Nothing's changed in at least 300 years around here. World Heritage Site? We're a shoo-in. Just got to work out a few of the details."

"Like what?"

"Got to pull a few artifacts together. Been interested in relics and the like since I was a kid. My dad was the manager here before me. Fellows from the university used to stay here in the summer. This is my collection." He waved a ringed hand at a display. "Got stuff in here the local boys collected. Tourists like to see bits and pieces in glass cabinets with labels. They'll pay big bucks to get in to see a display like that." He swung his arms wide at a lobby with a dusty umbrella tree in a pot, four orange armchairs that looked like some cat had used them as scratching posts, and a veneered coffee table covered in pizza-joint flyers. "Got lots of room right here."

I tried to make sense of Danny's scheme. It wasn't easy.

"So, you're telling me that the Treasure Trovers found things in their travels that *are* valuable? As in, World Heritage Site valuable?"

Danny raised his hands, as if to say, "Why not?"

"And you're hoping to get an elderly retired professor with poor eyesight to verify these treasures? Is that it?"

"Bingo, we got a winner," Danny said. He leaned in closer to me. "Got a feeling the clincher is something Percy's brought in tonight. Only a picture, mind you. He says the thing's too heavy to haul in here. But he checked it out online and showed me his research, the evidence. Could be there are pictures of a genuine Gasper's Cove Viking artifact down that hall. That crowd that settled in northern Newfoundland? They say after those Norsemen set up camp, they kept going. Off in a southerly direction, looking for vineyards. Kinda proves those jokers didn't understand much about climate. Anyway, I figure this is where they ended up. Heard rumors for years. Other fellows looked for evidence in the past, but it was Percy who tracked it down."

"What do you mean?"

"A rock, a stone, from at least 1000 bc. He found one." Danny was triumphant. "Word gets out, I'm going to add rooms to this place. I started digging a hole for a pool last summer." He snapped his fingers with another idea. "Get those people from Europe to come over, better build a sauna too."

"A rock?" I asked, stuck on the details. "Lots of rocks are old."

"Not like this one," Danny said. "What Percy says he's got is a genuine photo of the about-to-be-famous Gasper's Rune."

"A rune?" I asked. The word sounded familiar, but nothing more. "What's that?"

"Something the Vikings left behind," Danny said, with new-found authority. "The runes are symbols, like letters of the alphabet, and they were used to write in the stone. These rune stones marked graves to honor warriors, but a bunch of them were supposed to have magic in them, spells, curses. Good or bad power. It could go either way. Percy says the important thing was to treat a rune stone right so it wouldn't turn on you."

I felt a chill and looked back to check to see if the front door was open. It was closed. "And you know what to do with it?"

"Hundred percent I do," Danny said. "I do whatever is good for business. Always."

He stood aside and let a guest pass. The man, in his late thirties, was fit and tanned. He wore a sleek, black, high-tech, insulated winter jacket, zipped up tight to the neck, and had both a camera with a long-range lens and a pair of binoculars around his neck. A bright orange wool hat, like hunters wear, was pulled low over his face. His eyes were partially covered by long sandy bangs.

"Evening, Mr. Black," Danny said. "Cold one out there. Don't see weather like this in Atlanta. Must make you happy."

The man grunted, and his lip-balmed mouth formed a reluctant line, part smile, part grimace. Danny waited until the visitor disappeared through the door to the stairs before he leaned toward me and explained, "That fellow's from down south, Jason Black. He's a storm chaser, like on the YouTube. Not one of your more regular professions, and I don't think buddy there is much good at it. If he'd listened to the local weather, he'd know we're in for a mild winter. There's going to be nothing to chase."

CHAPTER FIVE

The weather for the rest of the week should settle down, thanks to high pressure. A storm will move over the Atlantic, but local models confirm it will miss us. CKGC, Voice of the Waves.

With Gareth in the safe hands of Percy and his group, I tried to think of how best to use the two hours until I had to be back to pick him up.

I called Kay.

"How do you feel about a visitor?" I asked. "I'm out and about and in the mood for tea."

"Oh, Mom, that sounds great. Maybe some other time?" Kay sounded distracted. "I promised Tristan I'd take him over to Drummond for dinner."

"No problem. Have fun." I mentally counted the days left before Kay went back. "Tristan seems very nice," I added.

This gave me my daughter's full attention. "He's cool," she said, "and he loved you." She giggled at something in the background, said a rushed goodbye, and hung up.

I'd geared myself up for tea and didn't feel like going home, being alone. Then I remembered the checks in my pocket. I was in Drummond already. My car knew where to go next.

Stuart was home.

He'd left his Christmas lights up, and in the early darkness of winter they were on. Stuart's street was famous over the holidays. Four years running, it had won the municipality's "Best Holiday Lights" contest. From November to the end of December, tour buses, many of them filled with seniors from Seaview Manor, drove slowly down his street so passengers could see the Santas, the sleds, the reindeer, windows, doors, roofs, and backyard sheds outlined with lights. Stuart had made large plywood cutouts of Santa and his elves, which he and his daughter, Erin, painted and propped up all over their yard, washed with color-changing spotlights. After Christmas, the cutouts came down, but the lights in the fir trees stayed. Stuart said he liked to look out at them when he did the supper dishes.

I parked beside a snowbank eaten and eroded by freezing rain. Here on the coast, winter came in freeze-thaw layers, ice over snow or, more dangerously, ice under snow. It didn't surprise me to see that the walkway to Stuart's front door had been snowblown into a neat high-walled channel or that salt to melt the ice, and sand to add traction, had been carefully spread over the front path. The same had been done to the sidewalk along the street, for the full length of the property. If anyone was going to slip and fall, it was not going to be in front of the residence of Stuart Campbell, consulting engineer.

My car was not the only one parked at the house. Right behind Stuart's station wagon in the driveway was a smaller car with a rack for carrying surfboards on its roof. I recognized it as belonging to Noah Dixon, a young freelance journalist and occasional radio broadcaster at CKGC. I wondered if Noah was here to see Stuart on news gathering or on more personal business.

Erin opened the front door. I'd known Erin even before I'd met her father. She and her friend Polly made friendship bracelets and jewelry for the Co-op. Now in high school, they also helped at our craft-making workshops.

"Hi, Valerie," Erin said, standing aside to let me in. "Did you get the earrings we left at the counter?"

"I did, thank you. They'll go quick online. Which is why I'm here." I opened my bag and took out two envelopes. "I have your commissions. One for you and one for Polly. You girls did very well during the Christmas sale."

Erin grinned. Her hair, a lighter brown than her father's, was cut in a stylish bob these days, so different from the French braids she wore when I first met her. I wondered if the hair came from her mom, someone I had never met. All I knew about Erin's mother was that she was a lawyer who lived in Halifax with a partner in her firm and that Erin visited them often. Stuart never mentioned his ex-wife, and I never asked. I didn't know the full story. I wasn't sure if I ever would.

I kicked off my boots. Stuart called out from the kitchen. "Who's that at the door?"

"Valerie. I got it, Dad. She brought money for me and Polly." Erin yelled back.

I heard a chair push back. Stuart appeared in the archway of the kitchen. Birdie, his Nova Scotia Duck Toller, pushed his way past Stuart's legs and ran up to me, his tail wagging so hard, the little dog swayed. Stuart smiled at me with his daughter's light-up-the-room smile. "Noah's here. We're talking winter tires. Come on in."

I followed Stuart into the kitchen and sat down. Stuart plugged in the kettle for tea.

"Was that your voice I heard on the radio?" I asked Noah. I liked the young reporter. He was friends with my sons, and I felt closer to them when we talked.

"You got it," Noah answered. "It's kind of a cash-flow thing while I'm working on a book on unsolved mysteries of Nova Scotia. I do the back shifts or cover when someone's away. Suits me, suits the station. I like doing the weather when I can. Us winter-surfer guys pay attention. Not that weather reporting is easy. So many of the models are wrong these days."

Stuart put a mug of tea down in front of me. It was one of his specials, a potent mixture of ginger, eucalyptus, mushroom, herb, and turmeric. He gave it to anyone who would drink it as part of his one-person flu-prevention campaign. I inhaled the steam in my cup. It smelled like the ointment my mother used to rub on our chests when we were sick.

"What do you mean, the models are wrong?" I asked Noah, reaching for a brownie on the plate in the middle of the table. Stuart liked a recipe that used black beans. They gave the brownies density; I gave him that. And Stuart wanted to make sure Erin had enough protein.

Noah watched me drink the tea. "Last summer, I talked to that old guy who comes here from Boston. You know, the one who set up the weather hut with instruments?"

I nodded. The "old guy" was a retired professor from Harvard who, during the season, was often in the store, buying supplies for his cottage. "So, what does he say?" I asked. I wondered if a nice chocolate icing would help the brownies.

"He told me most weather predictions are based on historical data, environmental expectations," Noah said. His own brownie was untouched on his plate. "But he also said that weather is changing everywhere so rapidly that none of that applies like it used to. That's why, despite all their computer imaging, mathematical models, and satellites, even Environment Canada has trouble knowing what's coming next."

"I can see that," I said. "They get it wrong a lot."

"But we don't," Noah pointed out. "Like they say down at the station, all news is local, and so is the weather. Last winter, the most accurate forecasting came from our own data, right here, our shed. It will be even better with the new app they got."

Stuart laughed. "*Sunny with a chance of flurries or cloudy with a chance of sun, except along the coast, where fog is expected and the snow will turn to freezing rain,*" he recited, describing the weather forecast most common in Nova Scotia from November to early April.

I tried to delicately extract a soggy herb leaf from between my front teeth. "If the winters are getting milder, that's fine with me."

Stuart stood up and took the plate of brownies to the counter. When he returned, he had a tin of oatcakes in his hand. "Help yourself," he said, snapping off the metal lid. "But listen, Val, don't get too complacent. Did you get the winter tires on your car?"

"Meant to," I confessed. "But I didn't get around to it. I have them in the basement at the store. I think the mice are back down there, so I've been staying clear."

"Those tires aren't going to do you much good there," Stuart said. "I'm glad to see you have the sense to drive the store truck. Heavier vehicle. Four winters on her. All-wheel drive. Keep doing that until you get the tires changed on your car." He paused as if reading some checklist in his head. "You got wood for the wood stove, don't you? In case the power goes out?"

"Yes. I've got lots left over from what you brought over in the fall."

"Right. Good. Salt for the walkway? How about candles?"

"Lots of candles. All decorative," I said. "From the Co-op. And I'm fully stocked on storm chips." These were what locals called snack supplies put away for snow days.

I wasn't sure if Stuart had heard me. His eyes had that unfocused look he got when he reverted to engineer mode. "Before next winter, let's look at a solar generator for you," he said. "I've got one for here. It's good if there are any issues with the grid. You don't want to worry."

I wasn't worried at all, but it was clear Stuart was. Behind him, at the counter, Erin rolled her eyes.

"Hey, is that Kay's boyfriend who's visiting?" she interrupted. "He's hot."

"Not a boyfriend," I answered. "A friend. He's staying at the Anchor. He seems very nice."

Noah's mug spilled tea when he put it down. "Boyfriend?" he asked. "Since when?"

"Not a boyfriend. A friend," I repeated. "I don't think they've known each other long. Maybe a few months?"

"Is he another vet?" Noah persisted. "Someone from school?"

"No, he isn't." Why did it matter? "His job, as far as I can tell, is podcaster."

"Can you make a living doing that?" Stuart asked.

"A podcast?" Noah asked, his back straight in Stuart's refinished oak kitchen chair. "Would I have heard of it? What's it called?"

"*Solved and Resolved*," I said. I was pleased I had remembered. I was about to explain it was about true crime when my phone buzzed in my pocket. I pulled it out and smiled.

"Darlene," I told the table. "Cuba. Do you mind?"

"No, go ahead," Stuart said, his eyes on Noah, amused. "Tell her I said hi."

"I will. Let's see what she says." I clicked open the message and read it out loud.

> I can't believe it. Mom just texted me about Percy at the motel. Do they know what happened?

I looked at Stuart, Noah, and Erin and shrugged. I'd talked to Percy not much more than an hour ago. He had seemed fine.

What about him?

Darlene hardly knew Percy. She was on her honeymoon. Why was she interested in him now?

You don't know!??

Know what?

I asked.

He's missing. They can't find him anywhere. And there's blood all over the snow.

CHAPTER SIX

I repeated that last line.

Noah was out of his chair. Phone in his hand, he hurried to the living room, making a call as he walked.

The young surfer who wanted to talk about my daughter was gone, the journalist was back.

Later.

I texted Darlene.

If I find out anything I'll let you know.

I added.

"Erin, don't you have some homework to do?" Stuart asked.

"Dad, I'm not a kid," Erin said, even though she was. "I'm old enough to hear everything." She sat down.

Noah walked back into the room. "As usual, the Gasper's Cove word-of-mouth news network is ahead of everyone else," he told the kitchen. "I talked to a buddy of mine who works the desk at the motel. I guess some of the guys at a meeting, including Percy, went out for a smoke during break time. It's cold. They didn't stay out long. When the rest of them came back in, Percy stayed outside. Someone had a question, so they went out to get him. That's when they saw blood all over a snowbank, but no Percy. They're looking for him now."

"Whoa." Stuart watched Erin's face. "What happened? Do they know?"

"No idea," Noah shrugged. "They called the RCMP."

"Did he slip and fall on the ice?" I wondered. "Hurt his head and wander off?" He'd seemed fine earlier this evening.

"No idea," Noah said, "but like I said, there was a mess on a snowbank. Someone was plowing the lot. Maybe some kind of accident." Noah caught a look from Stuart and glanced at Erin. He took his jacket from the back of a chair and shrugged it on. "I'm going over to the motel to check it out." He stopped at the doorway and turned back. "Hey, Val, next time you see Kay, say hello from me."

I nodded. Then, I remembered Gareth. "I better go too. I have that professor to pick up at the Anchor. I bet he wants to get out of there."

"I'll walk you out," Stuart said. He followed me to the front door, took my jacket out of the hall closet where Erin had hung it, and held it out so I could slide in my arms.

"Poor Gareth," I said. "Some introduction to Gasper's Cove! I'll talk to Danny, he's the manager. He'll know more."

Stuart took my hat from the bench in the vestibule and put it on my head. He kept his hands on my shoulders. "Stop right there," he said. "Repeat after me: This is none of my business."

"I know that," I said. "But I told Darlene I'd get her some information."

"Listen to yourself," Stuart said. "It sounds like Darlene is getting all the news she needs from her mother. You stay out of it." He put my scarf around my neck and pulled me closer. "Promise? Pick up this gentleman and take him back to the Inn. Then, go right home."

"I will," I said. "You have nothing to worry about." I opened the door and went out into the cold. My mind was whirling. Who was the snowplow operator? Could he hit and bury someone with his plow and not know it? It was a dark night. I bet the RCMP had forensics working the shovel of the plow, taking samples of the snow. That's what I'd do.

I took my keys from my pocket and got into the truck. Noah's car was already gone. The Anchor Motel was less than ten minutes away. I started the engine and turned up the heater.

I waited to let two cars by, and as they passed, I saw that onc was a truck with Georgia plates on the back. I turned into the motel's driveway. Officer Wade Corkum was crunching around the parking lot with two other Royal Canadian Mounted Police officers I hadn't seen before. A truck with a plow attached to the front of it was parked on the service road that led to the motel. There was no one in it. I suspected the driver had been taken in for questioning. I knew how these things worked—I'd had my own encounters with local law enforcement, once as a possible suspect, and a few times when Wade had asked me for my help. Secretly, I considered myself a member of some kind of RCMP women's auxiliary, not unlike the ladies who assisted the minister at the church. I didn't help law enforcement with bake sales, but I did what I could to help. As a sewing teacher and crafter, I knew how to see the possibilities others might miss in otherwise-ordinary materials. That could be useful.

And, I had to admit to myself, as I parked behind a large pile of snow left by the plow, I simply liked to know what was going on. The thing is that if you run a business in a small community, everything is your business. That's just how it is.

And I wasn't the only one who felt that way. There was already a small crowd on the sidewalk in front of the motel. Some were dog walkers organizing among themselves to find Percy, and some drivers-by who had stopped to check out the action when they'd seen the RCMP cruiser's flashing light. Most of the attention, I noticed, was directed at the truck with the two silver blades attached to its front like the prow of a ship. I saw Wade near the motel's front door. I waved. Wade and I had gone to high school together. Once a local hockey star, he now headed the local detachment of the RCMP. I felt our long acquaintance meant I could say anything to Wade. He didn't seem to feel the same way about me, so instead of waving back to me, he snapped the metal measuring tape in his hand shut and strode over, his face grim and official under his woolen tuque, not the flapped muskrat hat he wore in the extreme cold.

"Hello, Valerie," he said. "What are you doing here?"

"I'm here to pick up a guest," I said, "and take him back to the Inn. A retired professor here for a meeting." As I spoke, I tried to look past Wade's shoulder at another officer standing at a snowbank. I could see the red in the snow and a plastic bag in the officer's hand, like the ones used to collect evidence. "What's the story on Percy? Buried under the snow?" I raised my eyebrow and tried to give Wade a look that conveyed, as a person of some law-enforcement experience, that I knew there was more than Wade was letting on. The RCMP wouldn't zoom over to a parking lot over some man who couldn't have been missing for no more than an hour. That made zero sense.

Wade sighed, his breath making a cloud in the cold air that lingered while I waited for his reply.

"Where did you get this information?" he asked.

"Cuba," I said.

Wade looked at the stars.

"Darlene's on her honeymoon," I continued. "Are you charging the plow operator? Who was it?"

"Why don't you ask Darlene?" Wade turned to watch a second RCMP cruiser pull into the lot.

"I'm here, she isn't. That's why I'm asking you. For the details." I wasn't giving up. Darlene wouldn't want me to.

"Look, I don't have time for this," Wade said. "But if it keeps the local busybodies out of my way," he locked eyes with me, "I'll share some facts before you go on your way. There's some evidence of an altercation. That's the only reason we're here. Otherwise, we'd wait for him to turn up."

I looked around at the parking lot. A few vehicles moved out; a few came in.

"Is his car still here?" I asked.

"Yes," Wade said.

"Did you call the hospital?"

"Of course. Valerie, I know how to do my job. Nothing to see here. If Percy Skinner is missing, we'll find him. Why don't you pick up your visitor and go on your way?" A third officer joined us. Wade turned toward him and started to walk away.

"Who was driving the plow? I didn't catch it," I called after him.

The younger officer, who did not know me and should have known better, answered.

"Local fellow," he said. "Harry Sutherland."

Harry.

Why was I not surprised? The possibility that Percy Skinner was under a giant pile of snow somewhere around me suddenly seemed more likely.

Harry was a man who made mistakes. It was his most defining characteristic. He meant well, but Harry had come into the world significantly short of common sense. On the downward slope of his forties, he lived with his mother, considered to be the longest-suffering woman in Gasper's Cove and one who tried to rescue her son from himself. Harry did his best. He had made a career of unsteady employment and picked up work wherever he could find it. In the spring, he ran a garden center on the asphalt outside the Foodmart. Summers, he tended bar at the yacht club on the north side of the island. Winters, he drove the big machine that resurfaced the ice at the arena between hockey games. And when it snowed, he attached a plow to the front of his truck and cleared it for anyone who paid cash. That would be why he was here.

I could see Harry plowing into Percy but not hiding that fact. Something else had happened. I wasn't leaving the Anchor until I knew what that was.

I walked up to the front door of the motel. I passed Noah as he was coming out.

"Oh, hi, Val," he said. "Your guy's waiting for you inside."

"Good, thanks." It was luck I'd run into the reporter. "What's the story? I hear that Harry drove the plow. Where is he?"

"In some meeting room, giving a statement," Noah said. "They're holding the truck. That's all I could find out." Noah paused and looked at me. We thought the same thing.

"There's something they're not telling us," I said. I stepped into the motel lobby. Noah reached out to close the heavy door behind me, to keep out the cold.

"Couldn't agree more," he said, "but no one is talking."

The same could not be said for Gareth Davies. The elderly professor stood next to the reception desk, deep in conversation with an RCMP officer, who seemed relieved to hand the professor over and expedite his exit.

"Ah, Madam, how kind you are to retrieve me from this crime scene," Gareth said, walking over to the salt-encrusted mat at the door. "I offered my assistance, but the Royal Canadian Mounted Police said they have my number."

"Crime scene?" Gareth had my full attention. "What do you mean?" We went outside to my truck. With effort, I hoisted Gareth up to the passenger's seat, got in myself, and waited for an answer.

"I am not sure when the Mounties are making it public," Gareth said after he fastened his seatbelt, adjusted his tam, put on his leather gloves, and rested his cane between his knees. "But take it from me, Mr. Skinner was killed. After all, I am as good a near eyewitness as anyone there."

"You saw it?" I asked, shocked. "You saw someone kill Percy?"

"Shall I start from the beginning?"

"Please."

"Well, we both went out for a smoke." Gareth patted his coat over his heart, presumably at the pocket where he kept his pipe. "After the group approved their last minutes, I presented myself and my qualifications until interrupted by a motion to take a short break. That's when Percy, I, and a few others went out the side door to indulge our vice. This gave me a chance to elaborate on my career in academia. I told them Rollie, whom they all knew, was my best and my brightest student. They were interested, but it was too cold to remain outdoors. So, we all went back in. We thought Percy was right behind us. But"—Gareth paused dramatically—"he wasn't."

"I guess not," I said, turning up the truck's heater. I steered our way between the snow piles and out onto the road, moving cautiously into the lane that would take us to the causeway and home. The wind was picking up. A flurry of snowflakes, large and light, chased their way past my windshield to melt on the asphalt until the temperature dropped and turned them to ice. Driving would be treacherous.

"So, that's it? The rest of you went back into the motel. Percy stayed out to finish his smoke?" Details mattered. "And someone went back out to get him?"

"Give me time, Miss Rankin; I have a story to tell. As I said, I believe I am the last person, except for his killer, to see Mr. Skinner alive." Gareth tightened the scarf around his neck. "Our departure. Being the most senior of the group, I lingered. I'm past the time in my life when I rush for anything or anyone. As I left, I saw Skinner toss his butt into a snowbank, a nasty habit, and walk off. With a purpose, I'd say, like someone or something had caught his attention. I went back inside to make my contributions to the continuing discussions. Near the end of the meeting, someone came in and told us about the blood."

"The last time you saw Percy walk away," I persisted, "did you see anyone else there?"

"No, not that I could make out; however, my eyesight isn't as sharp as it was in my bird-watching days. Which reminds me, did I ever tell you about the time I spotted a painted bunting in the bush? I am one of the few amateur ornithologists in the province to ever have done so." Gareth smiled at the memory of this achievement. "I love birds. Which is why I am in full support of a laying flock at the Inn."

"Flock? At the Inn?" I asked. "Chickens?" I caught myself. This was no time for detours. "Never mind that now. Back to Percy. He walked off into the parking lot, but you didn't see why, or if, he was going to see someone?"

"Exactly. The parking lot is not well lit, but a few vehicles came and went. And there was the snowplow."

The snowplow. We were getting somewhere. A routine plowing job late at night, flurries, declining visibility. The big heavy shovel of the plow knocked Percy down before Harry saw him. This wasn't a crime; it was a tragedy.

"I am sure it was an accident," I said.

"An accident?" Gareth seemed surprised by the idea. "I think not."

"Poor Harry," I said, elaborating the image in my mind. "A dark night ..."

"Harry? A plow?" Gareth stared at me. "This was nothing that brutal. Mr. Skinner's death was, in my estimation, more subtle. The quantity of blood makes me feel there was a ceremonial quality to it, almost sacrificial."

A sacrifice? In a Drummond, Nova Scotia, motel parking lot behind a snowbank? Voodoo? Was this where the chickens came in?

"How do you know that?" I asked, as my tires started to skid. I moved my wheels away from the median. "The RCMP haven't even made a statement."

Gareth turned to look at me, the shoulder of his seat belt cutting into the fine wool of his coat. "I would expect a woman of a certain age to understand this, but at some stage of life, you become invisible. When the officer took my statement, along with those of everyone else at the meeting, I offered them my considerable experience in evidence analysis. He turned me down. I think he considered my age in that decision. However, being discounted as irrelevant gave me a particular opportunity to employ another of my research skills."

"Which is?" I turned the fan on the heater down to make sure I didn't miss any real facts that might be buried in Gareth's sentences.

"Data collection. I was always good in the field," Gareth said. "While I was waiting for you, I listened to the officers talk among themselves." He tapped his ear. "I'm less nimble than I was, and I don't see as well as I did, but my hearing is excellent. I know, I paid for it. The switch from analog to digital technology allows hearing aids to be calibrated for individual preferences. Mine are particularly good at cutting out background noise."

"Good to know," I said, "but back to Percy. What makes you think this was some kind of"—I struggled to find the right words—"symbolic murder?"

"They found a small knife in the snowbank. One of the officers said it looked like a stiletto, probably a term he'd heard bandied about. But my thoughts went elsewhere. The phase of the moon, February, being halfway between the winter and summer solstices, the ritual removal of the body. The grand return to Valhalla of the Einherjar, the warriors who fight alone. It all fits."

I tightened the grip of my mittened hands on the steering wheel. This was no time for the archeology professor to go academic on me. "I'm not sure what you mean," I said carefully, not wanting to encourage a lecture, "but to be clear, are you saying that Percy, wherever he is now, was stabbed?"

"Yes. By a knife, a sharp one, if it looked like a stiletto. Something like a Second World War trench knife, perhaps, or a Viking war dagger, if my theory is correct. If not, maybe a Highland dirk." Gareth considered the possibilities. "I wish I'd had a closer look. I was sure I saw something of that class in the display case in the lobby when I arrived. But that manager fellow says there were no knives in the collection." Gareth turned to look outside at the dark through the window. "Do you think the assassin brought his weapon with him?"

I had no answer to that.

CHAPTER SEVEN

For the rest of our drive to the Inn, I let Gareth talk. His descriptions of the history, appearance, and forging challenges of knife making, utilitarian, ceremonial, and military, washed over me while I considered Percy's death.

It was apparent that Gareth had done what most of us would when faced with unexpected situations: He had tried to reformulate it to fit his own experience. From that perspective, I could see why an archeologist would assume the knife the RCMP found was an older weapon. That said, I wondered if Gareth was right. Wasn't it odd that the president of the Gasper's Cove and Drummond Treasure Trovers had gone missing, possibly stabbed, in the middle of a meeting to discuss locally found artifacts?

Gareth expounded all the way to the Inn. I parked close to the front door and helped him up the steps. To the right of the porch, I was surprised to see the summer-patio floodlights turned on. In the middle of it, Rollie and Simon were constructing something that looked like a large child's playhouse.

Catherine opened the door for us and led us into the reception area.

"I heard," she said as a greeting. "My phone has gone off all evening. Strange news about Percy. Does anyone know what happened?"

I jumped in before Gareth could. Catherine liked her information direct and unembellished. "No idea. The RCMP are there."

"Oh my." Catherine gave me a long look. "I hope they find him and figure it out. I've had calls from people to tell me it was a hostage situation, and the Anchor Motel was shut down, and from others that Danny forgot to salt the lot, and if Percy had family, there would be a lawsuit."

"None of that," I said.

"My assessment is a killing of a ritualistic nature," Gareth offered, taking a deep breath, about to launch again into Ancient Knife 101.

I decided to divert him. "What are Rollie and Simon building?" I asked. "In the dark?"

Catherine closed her eyes. I noticed she had her winter jacket on. I wondered if she was outside to supervise the project or to complain about it.

"I am losing control of the management of this business," she said, as if stating a fact. "Yes, I know it's winter in Nova Scotia. And yes, I know we can be snowed in at any time. And yes, I know that self-sufficiency is something we should all be working toward. But at no time did anyone ask me if I wanted to start keeping *chickens* on this property. Five are arriving tomorrow. That's why Simon and Rollie are out there tonight—they're putting up a chicken coop. Winterized. We have electrical outlets out there."

"An excellent idea," Gareth said. "The medieval castles were always ready to maintain themselves. They were often under siege."

"I know the feeling," Catherine said. "Anyway, here come the builders."

The side door from the outside opened. A bank of cold air traveled down the hall, followed by Rollie and Simon, stamping their feet to deposit melting snow onto Catherine's clean, dry carpet.

"Done!" Rollie announced, his cheeks scarlet above his frosty beard. He reminded me of a little boy triumphant over the construction of a fort in the backyard. "I'll take the truck and pick up the girls tomorrow. I hear they are all good layers."

"Eggs are an excellent source of protein," Simon added. I noticed he was dressed in a padded camouflage print jacket and pants, as if blending in with the landscape was an essential part of chicken-roost building. "You need that for muscle mass. Which is important when there are fortifications to maintain."

"Solid thinking," Gareth agreed. "The medieval castles were completely self-contained."

Simon stopped rubbing off the fog on his glasses. "Castles?" he asked, interested. "I hadn't considered that. Rollie, what are your thoughts on building a moat?"

This was enough for Catherine.

"If you haven't noticed, Gasper's is an island, and we're surrounded by the waters of the Atlantic Ocean. I think we've got that covered," she said tightly. Looking for an ally, she picked up Dusty, the Inn's geriatric resident cat, which had been busily swiping business cards down to the floor. "But there's other news. At the motel."

Gareth stepped forward. "That's right, gentlemen. The meeting I attended was transformed by tragedy. I was a key witness, of course. During our break, the president of the group wandered off and disappeared. I believe he met an untimely end."

"What do you mean?" Rollie took the cat from Catherine, as if to protect her from the news. "What happened?"

"No one knows where Percy is, but there's blood in the snow and," I looked at Gareth, "apparently a knife. Wade's there."

"My goodness," Rollie said. "Percy is a harmless fellow, keeps to himself. I see him in the summer all the time. Down along the coast, looking at rocks."

The mention of rocks reminded me of something. "Gareth, didn't Percy have something to show at the meeting? Danny told me about pictures of something he called ... a what? A rune?"

Beside me, Simon reached into the pocket of his combat jacket and pulled out a phone. I watched as his thumb swiped rapidly over its surface and then stopped. He held up the screen for us all to see. Only Gareth didn't step forward to see it.

"Look at this," he said. "I ran into Percy last week. I was checking the perimeter of this island to do an inventory of escape routes in case a mass evacuation is ever necessary. I remember it was raining. Both Percy and I parked at the look-off, waiting for it to clear. I introduced myself—networking is an important part of crisis mitigation. Percy showed me the photo he took of a rock but wouldn't tell me where it was. I managed to sneak a picture, because it was interesting. Granite, with something scored on it. Percy said it was some kind of inscription. He was convinced it was an authentic Viking rune."

Gareth snorted. "Yes, he showed us the same photograph at the meeting. I would have preferred to examine the specimen in situ, to see where he found it, but my strong impression was that there were many reasons why that piece of stone was marked, but certainly not by Norsemen. Very unlikely. To date, there is no documented evidence of Viking settlements in this province. And believe me, if there was, it would be sensational. But highly unlikely. Unfortunately, our conversation on that issue was cut short."

"Who knows now, eh?" Rollie said. "The first thing is to find Percy and make sure he's alright." In his arms, Dusty reached up and patted Rollie's beard, as if in agreement. My cousin nuzzled the cat back. If they had both been able to purr, they would have. After a minute of this, Rollie remembered the other love of his life.

"Catherine, I think we and our guests need some tea. It's been quite the evening. Val, do you want to join us?"

I looked through the windows on either side of the Inn's large solid front door. Snowflakes spun around the porch light, like fireflies. "Thanks, but I think I'll head home before the roads get bad," I said. "Toby needs a walk."

"Fair enough," Rollie said. "We had the radio on when we were out working on the patio. They're not expecting much snow. It's supposed to clear up by the morning, but better safe than sorry."

Simon looked up from his phone.

"Right, the sewing class this week," he said. "I'll be there. I'm not sure what I should do for my very first project. I can't decide. An overcoat or maybe a kilt?"

Oh boy, I thought, my ladies are going to enjoy Simon.

I was halfway home and well into rehearsing a speech for Simon on how kilt-making was an art, not a beginner's project, custom-fitted and requiring at least eight yards of tartan, when my phone buzzed. I glanced at the seat beside me. It was a text from Darlene. Close to the look-off, I checked for nonexistent oncoming traffic, and I made a quick turn. I parked under a tall light to read.

What's the news on Percy? Mom says you were there.

I had to give my aunt Colleen credit: The Canadian Broadcasting Corporation was never this fast or this accurate.

Aren't you on your honeymoon?

I tapped back.

Better things to do?

I added.

George is right here. We both want to know what you found out.

OK. Harry was plowing the lot. Not sure that matters. Blood in the snow. They found a knife, but no Percy. Lots of stories.

😮 Get out of town!!! Where did he go?

I guess that's what everyone wants to know. Wade in particular.

George says this doesn't make sense. Random stuff doesn't happen back there at home.

No kidding.

What do you think? You always have ideas.

Darlene knew me well.

I don't know. It just happened. Give me time. So far, all I got is one professor who thinks it was a ritual killing.

🤨 You talking about that old guy staying up at the Inn? You might want to keep looking. Not sure he's that clued in.

George says go talk to Harry. He likes you.

She continued.

Not a bad idea. I'll keep you posted.

You better. ❤

I signed off and put my phone back on the seat beside me. Even with the car heater on high, I could hear the surf turning aggressive at the bottom of the cliff, just past the guardrail a few yards away. This was something I'd never liked about the look-off. When we were kids, we used to throw stones over the edge and watch them bounce down the cliff, that long, slow, sharp drop to the black water, where they would disappear forever.

I shuddered and turned on the radio.

> *Good evening, listeners. Light snow expected this evening, a total of 5 centimeters in some areas, easing off along the coast, more in high terrain. Should taper off overnight, but motorists should be prepared for winter driving conditions. High winds may pick up later. We all know gusts can toss loose objects into the air and cause injury or death. Folks, it might be a good idea to stay inside if you don't have to go out. Tomorrow will be calmer, with a mixture of sun and cloud with only a chance of light flurries.*

A better day tomorrow. Sun was good news. Over at the edge of the parking lot, I saw the small hut where CKGC collected the data for its reports. Originally erected to collect meteorological data for the navy, the small windowless brick building had been abandoned during the official move to scientific computer modeling and the objective information sent down from satellites. Local people were skeptical of forecasts produced by this new technology. Most still relied on the readings from this unassuming outpost high on a cliff. The instruments on the roof—the whirling cups of the anemometers measuring the wind, the weather vanes showing wind direction, the rain gauges, thermometers, lightning detectors, and barometers measuring atmospheric pressure—reminded me of my father. My dad had worked his whole career for the Nova Scotia Department of Natural Resources. Our backyard at home had been populated with many versions of the tools this remote weather station still used. I backed out and drove in closer to have a look, and to remember my dad.

I wasn't alone. An unfamiliar truck was already there, parked close to the little building, still running, emitting a white cloud of exhaust floating off into the night. The driver was outside, his orange tuque fluorescent in my headlights. When he saw me, whoever it was jumped back into the truck, as if he were making an escape, slamming the door, twisting in his seat as he backed up, charging past me, so close I saw the peach in the middle of a license plate that had come all the way from Georgia, snapping a connection into place in my mind, like a magnet, so strong I could almost feel it, so loud I could almost hear it.

And with it, a question.

I knew that hat. Why was Jason Black, a guest at the Anchor Motel, out here by himself, late at night on the look-off, when there was nothing to look at?

CHAPTER EIGHT

My students filed into the expanded sewing classroom we'd made near the front door of the store. A small group of women had signed up for *Tailoring for the Terrified.* A few were women who wanted to learn how to insert linings. Two were young mothers who wanted a night out of the house. The last student was my part-time employee, Darlene's mom, my aunt Colleen, there, like the rest of them, primarily to socialize.

Simon hadn't arrived.

While I arranged my supplies at the table at the front of the room, I listened to the chatter.

It had been four days since Percy's disappearance, and he was the topic of conversation. His home, a trailer in the woods, was deserted. No one had seen him at the Foodmart, the liquor store, the bus station, or on foot along any of the rural roads, which was the only way he could have traveled, since his car was still uncollected in the Anchor Motel's lot. The RCMP had looked for relatives or friends they could contact, but there didn't seem to be any. Percy Skinner, a man who had spent so much of his time searching for traces of lost lives, had vanished, leaving no evidence of his own. All that was left was a snowbank spattered with blood and a knife of indeterminate origin.

"I ran into Harry's mom at the Foodmart," one of the older ladies said, unrolling wool yardage, the paper pattern still pinned to it. It was a jacket she'd started in 1972. She claimed this was winter it would get sewn. "She says he's beside himself. He'd got a new plow for the truck, and the first thing everyone asks is if he used it to bury a body by mistake."

"Can you imagine?" The sewer next to her wound a bobbin. "If there's trouble, Harry is in it. But I heard they didn't find any blood on the plow, which they would have, since there was so much around, so he's off the hook, back in business."

"Not that there is much plowing this winter," one of the young women observed.

Her friend, who had managed to book herself out of the house at bedtime, adjusted the lid of her take-away coffee and snickered. "Environment Canada? They told us there would be big storms during hurricane season in September. Remember that? All those disappointed surfers who flew in? Ocean was flat as glass all fall."

"Who listens to them?" another sewer asked. "Only CKGC gets it right. I've listened to it a lot, in case there is any news on Percy. They'd be the first to know. Unless," she paused, pins in her mouth, "you know something, Val, you haven't told us."

The ladies in the room looked at me. Everyone knew I was there that day.

"No. You know what I know," I said with some regret. I wanted to know more.

"Is it true someone stabbed him in the back?" Colleen's best friend, a woman named Agnes, looked up from the instruction sheet for her pattern. Agnes had been a nurse and liked to talk anatomy, which she missed.

"Who knows?" I said. "They won't until they find Percy." Or his body, I wanted to add.

Colleen lifted her glasses to better see the eye of a needle. "Maybe he just took off," she said. "That man's an odd one. Always was, ever since the accident." She and Agnes exchanged a look.

"Accident?" I asked, my mind sifting back through community history. "You mean the one when they built the causeway?" I'd been a child when it happened. I remembered the sound of the sirens.

"That's the one. Your uncle was on that job." Sadness flickered across Colleen's face. "Massive loads of rock and fill went into that project, you have no idea," she said to the younger women. "Our side over here didn't want it built. The older people thought connecting the island to the mainland would ruin our way of life, but the powers that be went ahead with it anyway. I remember my own grandfather saying it was unnatural to cut across the water like that. Only time I ever saw him upset. He said you didn't want to mess with the ocean; it would always get back at you. Other people argued it would hurt the movement of the fish and affect the fishery. They knew what they were talking about."

"The catch around here was never the same after they built it," Agnes agreed. "Not the inshore."

"Back to the accident, and Percy. What happened on the causeway?" I looked at the big clock on the wall. Where was Simon?

"Oh, the place was overrun with people and companies we didn't know," Agnes began. "They brought in workers for the job, there were not enough locals. But a lot of the new people were inexperienced. And they were all pushed to get it done fast, not right."

"My husband was under terrible pressure. I remember that," Colleen said. "He kept telling me if they didn't slow down, they'd pay for it. He said that site was one big accident waiting to happen. And he was right."

Agnes nodded. "I remember the day. There hadn't been enough compacting or something on part of the causeway. One of the trucks went too near the edge before the road was ready. That set it off, like a landslide. It was chaos. There were men in the water, rocks on top of them. In the end, I think everyone was accounted for, but a few of the men were hurt real bad. Some couldn't work after that. They never forgave him."

"Him?" I asked Colleen. My aunt was bent low in front of her machine, thread in her hand, squinting. "Never forgave who?"

Colleen looked up. "Percy," she said. "It was him driving the truck. He's been living out in the woods ever since. Hiding out in the middle of nowhere in a trailer, trying to take care of himself by scavenging. There are many stories come out of that causeway."

Before Colleen could say more, there was a loud crash at the back of the store. She and I looked at each other.

"The birdseed," Colleen said.

We sold a lot of birdseed in the winter. Many of the locals, me included, put it out for the shivering blue jays, woodpeckers, swallows, and wrens that, for reasons of their own, stayed with us in the winter rather than fly south with their more sensible cousins. We had bags and bags of it in the store and kept it near the back door so it was easier for customers to carry out to vehicles parked in the rear lot.

"Shadow," I explained to the class. With Duck away for a week's vacation, Shadow was full-time at the building and increasingly restless. "She patrols the birdseed, looking for mice. It sounds like she's knocked over a shovel."

"Maybe we should check?" Colleen suggested.

She had a point. The store was officially closed. The front door was locked, but we'd left the back door open for the students and their machines. I picked up a glass measuring jug.

"I'll go," I said. "I need to get water anyway to fill up the irons." Tailoring required good steam for shaping the sleeve caps and flattening the edges of the lapels.

I left the classroom, went to the tiny bathroom beside the manager's office, filled up the jug, and then walked to the back landing.

There, I found a person in an insulated jacket and pants, boots laced halfway to the knees, bent over as he tried to gather dozens of car snow brushes and ice scrapers spread over the floor.

Simon had arrived.

His glasses were fogged over. A woolen hat and big gloves the size of oven mitts lay on the floor beside him. When he saw me, Simon struggled to his feet, staggering under the weight of a giant backpack strapped to his back.

"Smart," he said, waving a thin pale hand at the stacks of salt, seed, and sand. "To barricade the rear entry like this. Slow down any floodwaters or intruders."

"All part of a careful strategy," I agreed, collecting the long-handled brushes and putting them back in the plastic garbage can where they lived, upright with the plastic triangles of the ice scrapers on top. "What you got in there?" I asked, pointing to the load on his back. "The class is for an evening, not overnight."

"Good one." Simon had a laugh that was part snort. "Catherine lent me some sewing supplies and an old sewing machine. A Singer Rocketeer, she said. All metal," he added, pausing to wipe beads of sweat from his forehead. "Sixty years old."

It was a great machine. I was surprised Catherine had parted with it, but then again, she wanted Simon out of the Inn. I picked up the oven mitts and hat and handed them to Simon. "Welcome," I said. "Follow me. The classroom is out front."

As we walked through the store, I explained its history to my new student.

"My family opened Rankin's General over a hundred years ago," I explained, pointing to the beautiful pressed-metal ceiling and its many layers of paint, one added by each generation. "Originally, the business mainly sold supplies to the fishing fleet, all schooners then, and basic staples for the islanders. In the winter, when the island was iced in, we were all there was. They say in the rumrunning days, there was booze hidden in the basement. The local boys used to take it down and deliver it to gangsters who met them in boats just past the twelve-mile limit outside New York Harbor."

Simon nodded. "I heard about that. Didn't Al Capone used to come here?"

"Sometimes. Here and the South Shore. He came to sign up local ships. He did the same thing over on Saint-Pierre and Miquelon, you know, the islands France owns off the coast of Newfoundland?" I liked to talk about our past to visitors. "After that, we had the war, then some good years in the fisheries. But things changed. The causeway got built, and local people started shopping over in the big stores in Drummond."

"Progress," Simon observed, "isn't always what it's cracked up to be."

I could agree with that. When we arrived at the door to the classroom, I helped Simon take off his backpack and lift out the heavy sewing machine. "Yes. And it doesn't always turn out the way you expected," I said. "Take this Rocketeer. It was designed to look like a rocket, built to take off. The engineers at Singer were enamored with the space race and the future. They thought at the time that this machine, with its cams and multiple zigzag, would be the last word in sewing machines, that there'd never be anything better, more advanced. But you can't see ahead." I thought of our old cash register, the one Colleen stood behind most days. It was the original, ornate, scrolled, and painted gold. "I sometimes wonder what my ancestors would think. We've gone from selling sails to making our money selling road salt and quilts."

Simon pushed his glasses, now fog-free, up his nose. The thick lenses made his eyes large and earnest. "I get it," he said. "It's exactly what Darwin said." Simon unzipped his leaf-patterned jacket. Underneath was a fleece vest and, beneath that, a flannel shirt. No wonder his hair was damp with perspiration.

"That the fittest survive?" I asked. "Not sure that would describe Gasper's Cove."

"No, that's a fallacy. He never wrote that." Simon leaned in closer. "But what he *did* write would describe this community."

"And that is?" I asked.

Simon looked at the old floorboards, wide and worn down in the middle so they bowed like waves, and then back at me.

"What he *actually* said was it was the most adaptable, not the fittest, who survived. Those willing to do the hard things, to redefine, to keep going. That's what you people do best." Simon picked up the Rocketeer. "And that's why I'm here."

CHAPTER NINE

It turned out Simon didn't do much sewing that evening. Once he understood that actual skill was required to make a coat or a kilt, he settled for what he'd really come for—interviewing my students, particularly the seniors in the group. He was intrigued that these women had sewn so much for their large families.

"Sounds very sustainable," he said. "All that mending to prolong the life of a garment in a multigenerational household." He pulled a notebook from the pocket of his pants and wrote that line down. "The Japanese have a name for it: Boro. They stitch up worn clothing so they can keep using it."

"Do they now?" Colleen asked. "Here we call it fixing up the hand-me-downs."

"The curse of the last child," Agnes laughed. "I had some winter jackets that had been worn by six other kids before my youngest got them. I had to fight to get them on her."

One of the young mothers laughed. "Having something new for yourself was a huge deal in my family." She paused to read her phone and groaned. "A message from my husband. The dog literally ate the homework. What teacher is going to believe that?" She rolled her eyes and then looked at Simon. "Why did you come this time of year? It is so much nicer in the summer. That's when everyone else visits."

"That's right," her friend agreed, pausing with her seam ripper in her hand like a tiny weapon. This was the third time she had put the left sleeve in the right armhole. "We don't want to give you the wrong impression of the place."

The room murmured in agreement. During the summer, we shared Gasper's Cove with visitors, refugees from prosperity who wanted to connect with a simpler way of life they had never personally experienced. In the winter, we lived that life, alone with each other. It was a rhythm we were used to.

"I'm writing a book," Simon explained. "About surviving in harsh conditions."

Colleen laughed. "Well, if that's what you're looking for, Nova Scotia this time of year is as good as it gets. So far, the weather has been pretty good, but our winters are gray and dreary. That's why we're taking this class. We sew, quilt, knit, and craft our way through November to April so we don't lose our minds."

"Got it." Simon wrote that down, too, and then stood up to circle the room, taking pictures with his phone of the students' projects, lingering on the tailor tacks, clipped necklines, and the pressing ham on the ironing board. "What do you remember most about winters growing up?" he asked us.

"Bread bags in our boots to keep our feet dry," Agnes said. "Food out on the back porch to keep it frozen. My sister walking home from high school in her nylons. They froze right onto her legs. My mother was wild, poured warm water over her so the skin wouldn't peel right off."

"Frostbite," Colleen added," is always a problem. I haven't had any feeling in my toes since the year of the white mice."

"The year of what?" Simon's eyes were wide.

Colleen laughed. "Sorry, a local expression. It means 'a long time ago.' The year of the white mice happened when?" She looked to me for clarification.

"1815," I answered. "There was a plague of mice in the province that ate all the food put away for the winter. It was like a famine. People got real superstitious about it. They said it was nature's revenge for changing times, for the new settlers coming in." I reached down and stroked Shadow, who had joined us in the classroom and was quietly batting a spool of thread across the floor. "That's why we have cats."

Simon scribbled in his notebook. "Great stuff," he said. "Speaking of food supplies, these days if you get caught in an emergency, what do you do?"

"We'd go down to the basement," Angus shrugged. "Everyone around here cans. And we all have chest freezers. We've got to be ready. Meat for the winter. Death ham."

I didn't think Simon's eyes could open any wider. "Death ham?" he breathed.

"You got to have them," one of the crafters said carefully, her mouth full of straight pins. "In case someone passes unexpectedly. To cook up and take over to the family with a big dish of scalloped potatoes. It's what you do."

"You have to understand," Colleen explained. "Maybe it's the climate we live in. A family has to be prepared. And you got to remember how short our growing season is. We don't want to waste anything either."

Simon put down his pen. "You mean you make jams? Jellies?" he asked.

"Yes, some of that." The woman next to him unpinned the paper pattern pieces from her project, a shirt dress in bright synthetic plaid. She had come to terms with the fact she was three sizes larger than she'd been in the 1980s and had decided to piece the fabric together to make a dog bed. "Blueberry, strawberry, and rhubarb jam. Good to have on hand to give to the neighbors at Christmas. Crab-apple jelly, if you have a tree. Chowchow, mustard pickles, pickled beets, beans, and the regular stuff. Peaches, tomatoes, and whatever is extra."

"My grandfather was a big hunter," one of the younger women volunteered. "They always put up moose meat and deer ribs. They bottled fish too."

"A lot of that around here," I explained to our urban visitor. "Everyone has a pressure canner. Lobster, because there's so much of it. Smelts, but they get those ice fishing too. I like smoked salmon and mackerel."

"Slow down," Simon was writing as fast as he could. "Mackerel?"

"Much better taste than salmon, in my opinion," a student struggling with slippery lining fabric added. "My dad used to keep an old fridge out back to smoke it in. Took out that freon stuff, put the fish on the racks, ran out an extension cord, and rigged up an element to heat up a can of wood chips. He used to smoke cheese out there too."

"Cheese?" Simon asked. "You made your own?"

"Once you got the rennet, it's not hard," Agnes explained. "Though some of the farmer's cheese they make down the shore is too stinky for my taste. The old people like it. I took some out to my aunt at Seaview Manor yesterday." She stopped to smile at me. "I ran into your daughter there, Valerie, with that nice young man. He had a taste, and he said he liked it."

"He was probably lying, being polite," Colleen told her. "I won't have the stuff in my house. I can't take the smell." Colleen's bobbin was empty; she paused while she rewound it. "My mother told me they'd been over at the Manor. It was nice of them to visit."

"I didn't know they were there," I said, although I wasn't surprised. Bernadette, Colleen's mother and Darlene's grandmother, lived in the Manor. Kay always made sure she saw her when she was home.

"Oh, yes," Colleen continued. "They stayed and had quite the chat. She told the boyfriend all the old stories. Mom thought he was a lovely young man."

"Friend, not boyfriend," I corrected. "What do you mean, 'chat'? What about?" Simon put down his phone and waited for Agnes's answer with me.

"Oh, the history of Gasper's Cove and some of the visitors we had over the years. Kay told him my mother used to take in boarders, a whole lot of sport fishermen," Colleen continued. "I remember that bunch. All they talked about was fish. Some of the others who stayed with us were more interesting. It was like an education in the house for us growing up. Let me see. ... There was a photographer once, a man from Scotland researching selkies—you know, half women, half seals, sort of cold-water mermaids? He was our favorite; he told us stories full of fantasy and legends. We also had a few biologists and historians stay with us over the years, but they were duller."

"I didn't know Tristan was interested in local history," I said. Here I'd thought he had come over to be closer to my daughter.

"I think it had to do with his work," Colleen said, walking over to the ironing board to shape a sleeve cap. "A biography maybe? That part wasn't clear. He said the project was in its early days. All I know is that he was working on something called 'The Lost Years,' whatever they would be, and for some reason, he thinks he might find them here in Gasper's Cove."

When the class was over, I ushered my students, Simon included, out the back door and locked it behind them. I was standing at the window, watching them all drive away, when my phone rang.

It was Kay.

"Hi, Mom, can you talk? Is your class over?" Kay sounded nervous. I wondered why.

"Just finished," I said. "How have you been?"

"Busy," Kay said. "Tristan wants to see everything and meet everyone, but we have this weekend free. Why don't you come over here for dinner at Darlene's house, to catch up." There was a murmur in the background. "Tristan says he'd love to cook for you. Saturday at 7:00?"

"Great," I said. I was talking to my child, but it all sounded formal. "What should I bring?"

"Nothing, just yourself," Kay said. "And we were thinking of asking someone else. Maybe Stuart. What do you think?"

I wasn't sure what I thought.

Stuart and I weren't exactly at ask-them-together status. I was surprised Kay thought we were. "And Erin? Stuart's daughter?" Kay continued. "She was so cute at the wedding. Too bad Darlene and George are still in Cuba. Tristan would love them too. He loves a party."

It seemed to me that there wasn't much Tristan didn't love. I wondered if that included my daughter. An idea sparked in the back of my mind. "If you want someone else to invite, how about Noah? He and Stuart are friends. Erin really likes him." Something told me I might need a wingman at this event.

"Sure," Kay said slowly. "He and Tristan could talk surfing and new media, that would work. I'll call him."

"You do that," I said. "And if you change your mind and want me to bring anything, let me know."

"Mom, it's fine."

When Kay hung up, I realized I was looking forward to this dinner. I was curious about this podcaster with the unidentifiable accent. Why was he so interested in our little community? And more to the point, exactly whose lost years was he hoping to find? As Kay's mother, I had to be careful not to be rude and ask too many questions.

But a local reporter, someone like Noah Dixon, could.

CHAPTER TEN

Dinner was elegant. That was the best way to describe it.

Stuart and Erin picked me up. Erin, now in her first year of high school, had dressed up for the dinner in wide-legged pants, a tiny camisole, and a short pink cardigan I was sure her father had made her put on to cover it up. There was a hint of a blue streak in her blond hair. I noted her expertise with eyeliner. It was time I stopped calling her one of my *junior* crafters.

"Nice earrings," I said to her when I climbed into the car. Stuart's car amazed me. The rubber mats on the floor were gravel and salt-free. There was a clip-on dog harness on the plaid blanket protecting the back seat and a net between the front and back so Birdie, Stuart's little red dog, wouldn't fly forward at the sudden stops a prudent driver, like Stuart, never made.

Erin flicked her head. The multicolored beads at her ears swayed. "Thanks. Chandelier-style. I'm making them for grad and wedding season. What do you think?"

"Bring them to the Co-op." Erin's jewelry was a big seller. "They'll fly out the door."

"Talented daughter you got there," I said to Stuart. Next to me, I saw the flecks of snow on his hair, mixed in with the beginning of the gray.

"Tell me about it," he said, "and your daughter too. A vet. Your kids have all done well. Now, this guy we're going to have dinner with tonight—what do you know about him?"

That was a very good question.

"Let's see. They met at a party in the fall. Not sure what his background is, but being a podcaster seems to be his job. Is that a job?" I asked.

"Absolutely, " Erin spoke from the back seat. "Is Kay going to marry him?"

"Erin," Stuart glanced at his daughter in the rearview mirror. "Take it easy. These things take time to develop. People want to get it right."

Erin snorted. She turned her face away and began scratching designs in the mist on the inside of the car window. "Not everyone is like you, Dad, and waits for, like, forever, even when they've made up their mind."

Stuart had nothing to say to this, and neither did I. The whole car was silent all the rest of the drive to Darlene's house.

Tristan was a careful cook, arranging the portions with an attention to detail that would have made any crafter proud. The first course was a single scallop, swirled with aioli mayonnaise, with one tiny sprig of dill, sprinkled with something that looked like saffron but, knowing Darlene's spice rack, was more likely ten-year-old turmeric. Forty minutes later, a spoonful of parsnip, the suggestion of a lamb chop, and a shaving of raw carrot followed this. After we'd worked our way through that, Tristan presented each of us with an ice cube of frozen lemon to cleanse our palates.

Next to me, I felt Erin kick her dad's leg under the table.

Cleansed, we waited for dessert. When it arrived, it was two strawberries (picked in California sometime before Christmas, but the best the Foodmart could do at this time of year) outlined with a figure eight of chocolate sauce and a single long haul–transported mint leaf, trying its best.

I thought of the hamburger-and-macaroni casserole at home in my fridge.

We had sat down at seven-thirty.

Kay brought in the tea at ten o'clock.

This gave us time to talk.

"I listened to your podcast," Noah said to our host. Noah wore a thick Aran sweater I knew his mother had knit him, jeans, and gray woolen work socks on his feet. Like all good locals, his footwear had come off as soon as he entered the house. Kay wore felted wool slippers. Tristan wore soft black leather shoes to match his black jeans and black cashmere turtleneck.

"Interesting stuff," Noah continued. "Sounds like you travel a lot. Where do you get your leads?"

"Here and there." Tristan held up a cut-glass decanter that I recognized as a wedding present from one of Darlene's new Greek relatives. "Something to go with your tea, Valerie?" he asked. "Beautiful dress. I can't believe you made it."

"Tea's fine," I said, pleased he'd noticed the dress. It was a fine crepe red wool that had eased into the princess seams well. I'd lined it with china silk. "I got the fabric when I visited Kay in Scotland. I'll go back for graduation."

My words lingered over the table. Kay and I hadn't talked about what she would do when her course was over. What did Tristan's visit mean? Would she stay in the UK if they became a couple? I opened my mouth.

Stuart cut me off.

"Right," he said, putting his folded napkin on the table. One of Darlene's cats was on Erin's lap. Both she and the cat were eyeing a solitary scallop on a plate on the counter. "Tell us about your studies, Kay. Your mom told me you started with birds, but that's changed?"

"That's right." Kay loved to talk. She and I had that in common. She also had my dark, almost black, curly hair and fair skin that burned in the sun. "I wrote my undergrad thesis on epilepsy in chickens. It's a real problem, particularly in commercial flocks, less so in backyard hens. The research was interesting. There was a good database. But it didn't feel like enough. So, I switched to small-animal behavior. Dogs and cats."

As if on cue, an old tabby with one missing ear rubbed himself against the leg of Kay's chair.

Tristan laid a hand on Kay's shoulder and squeezed it. Noah got up, took his cup to the sink, and rinsed it out.

"That's Kay. Loves her animals," Tristan looked around Darlene's little bungalow. "Lots of them here."

My daughter's cheeks were pink. "Rescues," she said. "My aunt and I more than love animals—we respect them. Most people," she glanced at the podcaster, "underestimate animals."

"No kidding," Erin agreed, returning from Darlene's mauve and white bathroom after the meal with a new layer of gloss on her lips. "Noah taught our dog how to surf."

"Not exactly surf, more like chase the board," Noah corrected. "Nova Scotia Duck Tollers are water dogs," he explained to Tristan. "They have a double coat. I hear you surf too. Do much in the winter?"

"Some," Tristan answered.

"Where?" Noah asked.

"Couple of places," Tristan said. "I don't have the time you do to surf, Noah. I understand you write and do some reporting. Lucky you."

"Thank you," Noah said. "And yes, I write and work as a journalist. For the radio station and for *The Lighthouse Online*."

"He's good," Kay interrupted. "Noah has won awards for some of his writing."

"Good for you, man," Tristan said, raising a glass. "What kind of work? Community events? The old hatch, match, and dispatch?"

"Some," Noah said, evenly. "I cover crime too. You'd be surprised what can happen in a small community like this one. Not everyone or everything is what they seem. You know?"

"Absolutely," Tristan said. I noticed Stuart's eyes were on Kay. "That's the basis for what I do, as I'm sure you know, if you have listened to the podcast. I go deep; my kind of journalism is about finding things local people might overlook."

The table went quiet. We listened to the ticking of the clock in the kitchen.

I decided it was up to me, as resident mother, to divert this conversation.

"So, Tristan," I said, "some of the ladies in my sewing class tell me you are writing a biography?"

Tristan shrugged. "Ah, they said that, did they? So far, I'm doing a bit of tire kicking—I do the same thing everywhere I go."

"How does that work out for you?" Noah jumped back in. "Didn't I hear something about some harassment charges? Invasion of privacy?"

Tristan grabbed an indulgent smile from nowhere and put it on his face. "I see you know how to Google," he said. "Great research technique."

Kay got up, took plates into the kitchen, and turned the tap on full force.

Stuart looked at her, stood up, and pulled my chair out. The evening had run its course.

"Time we got home," Stuart announced. "Wonderful meal, great company." He looked at Erin. "But for some of us, it's a school night."

"Yes. Very sophisticated," I added, aware of Stuart's hand on my back, steering me away from the table. "Beautiful food. Thank you so much." I went into the kitchen and hugged my daughter, and then Tristan. "Talk to you tomorrow, Kay," I whispered before I put my hand on Tristan's arm. "Thanks again."

Out in the hall, I heard Stuart open the louvered door of Darlene's front closet. That was my cue to join him. Stuart, his parka already on, held out my coat and then Erin's. Noah joined us and, while he waited for me to get on my boots, took one last look at Kay in the kitchen. He then turned and held my arm as we followed Stuart and Erin down the icy steps. Behind us, Tristan and Kay came out to stand at the top of the steps to watch us all leave.

One hand in his black jeans pocket, Tristan called down to Noah. He had put his other arm around Kay.

"See you later. Remember, you can't believe everything you hear, bro," he said with a wink.

Noah paused on the last step and turned around. "Don't worry, man," he said. "I don't."

Stuart let the car heat up before he backed out of Darlene's driveway.

"That went well, don't you think?" I asked him. "Tristan liked my dress."

Stuart turned to stare at me. "You have got to be joking."

I had no answer, so I shrugged.

"Dad, Dad," Erin reached her hand to shake her father's shoulder. "When we get home, can we order a pizza?"

"Not a bad idea," Stuart said. "I have to walk Birdie first."

"Fine," Erin said, "this is my idea: Valerie can stay and walk the dog with you. I'll wait for the pizza"—she had her phone out and was already reading a menu—"then we can all eat together."

"I'll consider it," Stuart spoke to his daughter through the rearview mirror, as he eased out of the driveway and onto the street. "That was a very nice dinner. Food like that is a lot of trouble to prepare."

"Oh, Dad, I know. I'm not being rude, but it was like more of an appetizer than a dinner, if you know what I mean."

"All right. Order the pizza." Stuart glanced sideways at me. "Val, you want to stay?"

"For a bit," I said. "I took Toby out earlier. He'll be fine."

"Good." Erin read from the backseat. "How does the extra-large family deal with medium garlic fingers and two liters of something to drink sound?"

"Perfect," her father said. I thought so too.

The temperature had not fallen as expected. In fact, by the time Stuart, Birdie, and I were as far as the community mailbox at the end of the street, the falling snow had softened into cold rain. By morning, much of the postcard-ready snow would be gone, turned into pitted ice, exposing patches of frozen yellowed grass and road gravel along the edges of sidewalks already cracked by the province's freeze-thaw cycle.

None of that bothered Birdie.

The little dog was well insulated, both by his waterproof coat and by every dog's conviction that today was the best day of his life. He bounded ahead of us as we walked, up and down the icy snowdrifts, cracking through them like a spoon on the caramelized sugar of a crème brûlée, falling through until the snow was as high as his chest, and then leaping back into the air to do it all over again.

"You know," Stuart said, taking my mittened hand so I wouldn't slip, "sometimes I wonder if I needed a quieter dog, say, like Toby. But then I look at Birdie"—the little dog heard his name and looked back at us, wagging his tail so hard his whole back swayed—"that face. He's so cheerful, so delighted to be here." Stuart stopped walking. He had something important to say. "You know what his favorite word is?" he asked.

"Treat?" I suggested. That was the most important word in Toby's golden-retriever vocabulary.

"No." Stuart stepped off the curb and onto the street "It's *home*. When we're out walking and I say, 'Let's go home,' there's an extra spring in his step. It's the best place in the world to him. I know how he feels."

I squeezed Stuart's hand. The rain was now sleet. "Maybe we should head back?" I suggested. "The food will be there."

"Good idea."

We turned around and made our way back to Stuart's house. By the time we were there, the sleet was falling hard, pinging as it drove into the pavement around the streetlights. Ahead of us, I saw Stuart's yard was already exposed. Ringed by snowbanks, like the edges of crust on a pie plate, frozen bent grass in the center, burlap-cloaked shrubs, standing on each side like a knife and fork, next to an arrangement of three boulders at the corner where the walkway met the sidewalk.

I was about to ask Stuart if I could give Birdie a dog treat I felt in my pocket, when the sheen of the sleet caught a texture, like carving, on one of the standing rocks.

I let go of Stuart's hand. I stepped closer.

I knew it.

"Where did you get that stone?" I asked. The freezing sleet dripped down my face and fell off my nose like raindrops. I didn't care. "Do you know what I think it is?"

"Granite?" Stuart asked. "It is everywhere in this province. Nothing special."

"You've got that wrong," I said. "This rock is so special, I think Percy Skinner was killed and vanished over it. That's a lost Viking rune you got there, right in your front yard."

CHAPTER ELEVEN

Before Stuart could say anything, his front door opened. Sanding in a halo of light, Erin looked out.

"The pizza's here," she yelled. "Dad, Valerie, Birdie is soaked. What are you looking at out there in the rain? People will think you're crazy." She checked the street to make sure no one from school had seen us.

"It's nothing," Stuart spoke quickly before I could talk. "Did you set the table?"

Even from where I was, I could see the eye roll. "Whose daughter am I?" Erin asked. "Of course I did. I put out napkins too."

Stuart laughed and unclipped Birdie from his leash. Tearing ahead of us, I could see him push past Erin to shake himself, splattering water and ice all over the off-white walls of Stuart's entry. As I crossed the threshold, I caught the smell of the pizza, cardboard boxes, and garlic. I was glad we had a teenager there to order garlic fingers. They were a local specialty, not very glamorous: fingers of crust covered in melted cheese, eaten dipped in donair sauce, a combination of canned sweetened condensed milk, vinegar, and garlic powder.

I thought of Tristan. Some of us are made to have our palates cleansed. And others of us are born to wipe donair sauce from our chins.

It was later, halfway into supper, that Stuart returned to the subject of the relics in his front yard.

"Define *rune*," he said to me, reaching for a paper napkin.

Before I could answer, Erin did.

"Dad, didn't they teach you guys anything in school? Runes are message tablets. The Viking explorers left them everywhere they went."

"First I've heard of anything like that around here," Stuart said as he picked up another large slice of pizza.

"That depends on who you ask," Erin said. She slipped a garlic finger under the table to the wet, red dog waiting there, convinced no one could see him. "My teacher is from down in Yarmouth. They have one there."

"Do they now?" Stuart folded up the big pizza box and stood up to take it to one of the two recycling bins he kept near his back door.

"Yes. It's called the Yarmouth Rune." Erin lifted her eyebrows at me, as if to ask whether I could believe how uninformed fathers were. "You must know about it," she said. "Everybody does."

Stuart returned to the table, gathered our plates, and stacked them, cutlery on top. "I don't. Enlighten me."

"I did a project on this in junior high," Erin explained. She cleared her throat, took a sip of her drink, and composed herself on her chair, ready to repeat her class presentation.

"It was discovered in Yarmouth, Nova Scotia, in 1812. It was heavy, about 400 pounds. There were letters on it. A few people thought the symbols were Greek or made by the Mi'kmaq. Somebody said the marks were natural, but nearly everyone else believed it was written in something called Old Norse, done by the Vikings more than a thousand years ago. And it wasn't the only rock with markings in the area." She paused to let the significance of this sink in. "Some expert said it was made by Leif Erikson, which was cool. Except for one problem."

"What was that?" I asked.

"The man didn't know how to read Norse," Erin explained. "I guess he was hopeful. There's no for-sure evidence that the Vikings came this far south. Maybe they did. Maybe they didn't. No one knows for sure."

"Where's this stone now?" Stuart asked.

"It was in the Yarmouth library for a long time, but now it's in the town museum," Erin said. "It might be real, or it might be what the teacher called a hoax. No one knows for sure, and that's what makes it interesting."

"Back to your front yard," I said. "Stuart, where *did* you get that stone?"

"It was in the fill Harry brought over to cover the trench after we put in the new waterline to the house." Stuart put on the kettle for tea.

Harry and his truck. They were everywhere. "And where did Harry get the fill?" I persisted.

"You'd have to ask him." Stuart's back was to me as he looked in his fridge for the milk. He found it and turned around to face his daughter. "Valerie thinks that one of the boulders we put in when we landscaped looks like a rune. What do you think of that?"

Erin shrugged. "Could be," she said. "People are interested in it. They stop on the sidewalk and stare at it. Probably wondering why we don't grow flowers like normal people."

Stuart stopped. "We do have flowers," he said. "Native species, for the bees. Besides, I haven't noticed our yard attracting attention. Who are you talking about?"

"Dad, chill out. You know, a man."

I leaned in. I had an idea. "What man, Erin?" I asked. "Was it Danny Dwyer? I know he's interested in artifacts."

Erin looked puzzled, then her face cleared. "The one from the motel who comes to our games? Who sponsors our volleyball team? No, not him. It was that old guy who walks the beaches with the metal detector."

"Percy Skinner?" Stuart asked.

"Yeah, that's his name. He's nice," Erin said. "He didn't do anything bad. He came by a couple of times to look."

"Stuart? I should go home and see Toby." I felt Erin watching us. "Can I see you in the hall?"

Stuart and I stood in front of the closet, Birdie between us. Stuart handed me my damp mitts and hat that he had draped over a chair in front of the pellet stove in the living room.

"Okay, what's going on?" he asked. "Why this sudden interest in my yard? Don't tell me you're going there again."

His tone annoyed me. Being told what to do didn't bring out the best in me. Being told not to do something brought out the worst.

"What do you mean, 'going there again'?" I knew what he would say next, and I was irritated in advance.

"You get these ideas. There's nothing more in my front yard than a rock that was in the fill. Nothing unusual there. Put a shovel anywhere in this province, and you'll hit a boulder. Why do you think we blast before we start new construction?"

"There were marks on that rock out there. I saw them."

"Have you ever seen the teeth on the bucket of a front-end loader?" Stuart asked. "The fill came from the hole they dug at the motel for some swimming pool. If you saw any cuts in the rock, they were made by an excavator, not Vikings." Stuart paused to zip up my parka. "Where's all this coming from, anyway?"

"I'm not a toddler, you know," I said, sounding exactly like one. I undid my jacket, and I zipped it up again, myself. Very impressive. "Your own daughter told you that Percy, the missing president of a band of artifact hunters, came by to look at your front yard. We all know why."

"We all don't," Stuart said. "You and who else?"

"Simon Broadbent, the prepper who's staying at the Inn. Percy showed him the picture of a rune. Maybe it's a picture of that stone out front. Visual evidence of something Percy saw and felt mattered. Simon will back me up. He's educated. A published author. Of three series," I added.

Stuart crossed his arms but smiled at me.

"A series? What kind?"

"Young adult fantasy." I realized how this sounded. "But he's moving into nonfiction, doing research on how to prepare for the coming apocalypse."

"Right." Stuart reached past me and straightened the coats in the closet, turning around some of the hangers so they faced the same way, an important task that couldn't wait. "Tell me more."

"Simon said Percy told him the rock in the picture on his phone was made by Vikings."

"And he took this picture of this archeological find in my yard?" Stuart bent down to straighten up the boots on a spotless rubber mat, as if he didn't want me to see his smirk, which I did anyway.

"I don't know for sure," I admitted. "He wouldn't tell Simon where he took the picture. But Simon showed me a copy. Your rock, and that one, look the same."

Stuart stood up and looked around. Maybe he had misplaced his duster. "You sure?" he asked.

"I'm going to find out more," I said, "and get back to you." I liked how mature that sounded. "There's more to this than we know." I forced my feet into my soggy boots and pretended that was a pleasant thing to do. "In the meantime, if I were you, Stuart Campbell, I'd cover up that rune in the front yard before someone else finds out you have it."

I wasn't sure if Stuart heard me. I called out a goodbye to Erin and then walked out the front door and onto the steps.

The sleet had stopped.

CHAPTER TWELVE

The next morning, I decided to text George Kosoulas before I tracked Harry down. I had questions only someone with tables at Gasper's Cove's sole restaurant could answer.

I found George's number.

> Sorry to bother you on your honeymoon.

I was doing exactly that.

> Quick question. Were Percy Skinner and Danny Dwyer close?

I waited. Bubbles appeared on the screen.

Nice to hear from you too Valerie. Darlene says hi. Duck's here in Cuba! How's that for luck? Did Percy turn up?

> Not yet.

I answered.

Geez. What do you want to know about Danny and Percy? And why?

A reasonable question. I dogged it.

Did they ever have lunch together at the restaurant?

Everyone eats at our place. Again, what's up?

I hesitated. A text was not long enough to get into Leif Erikson.

Wondering if maybe they had a scheme going on. Harry was in on it. Got out of hand maybe? Wondering what happened to Percy.

Whoa. Why are you even thinking about this?

Because.

I wrote. That cleared things up.

There was a pause. I figured George must be talking to Darlene.

OK. Harry? His middle name is Scheme. Him and Danny eat together. With Percy? Never.

Interesting.

I wrote back.

Watch yourself kid.

The bubbles were back.

Darlene wants to talk to you. Me and Duck are off to happy hour.

The screen went quiet, then came to life.

Are you nuts?

I knew then I was talking to Darlene.

No. Worried.

About???

It wasn't like Darlene to miss happy hour. I knew if I was worried, that would worry her.

Not sure. Everything. Percy. This friend of Kay's.

The RCMP will find Percy. Take it easy.

More bubbles appeared on the screen.

Friend? Boyfriend?

Friend as far as I know.

Sooo, what about him?

He seems interested in everybody else but doesn't want to talk about himself.

I reread what I'd written. It sounded foolish. Darlene thought so too.

Maybe you're thinking too much. About things that are none of your business. What does this friend do again?

Podcaster? What do we know about that?

Not much.

Darlene had a point.

Means he's a news guy. Like Noah?

She continued.

Noah didn't like him.

I tapped back.

There was a pause. Darlene was thinking.

Stay out of it.

This was her standard advice to me about my adult children.

Why did you text George?

She asked.

I'm thinking about a rock. What if it's connected to Percy?

Stop this!

I could hear the tone of Darlene's voice in the words on the screen.

The only rocks that matter are the ones in your head. I am on my honeymoon. Home soon. Do nothing.

My brain was well over the speed limit. What if I was the only person who understood what was going on? What if something happened now to Danny, Harry, or, worst of all, Erin or Stuart? My phone beeped. Another line from Darlene.

> I have a margarita waiting. Promise you'll mind your own business.

I promised nothing.

Darlene wouldn't have believed me anyway.

The thing was, and I hadn't told her, that I felt guilty. I couldn't get the image of the little man in the motel hallway out of my mind. The loner who had disappeared and no one missed. He had something to tell me, that I was the only one he trusted with his secret. I couldn't shake the feeling that, somehow, I had let him down.

This all had to do with that rock. The one in Stuart's yard, the one in Percy's photo. I could feel it. My mind was made up. I dropped Toby at the store. I left him looking for Shadow, still off on her hunt, and I headed over the causeway to Drummond.

I arrived at the Anchor Motel just as a tourist bus pulled out. Danny was in his street shoes on the salt-covered sidewalk, waving it away. Only when the bus was out of sight did he turn and go back into the building. I parked and followed him inside.

"Love seniors," Danny said when he saw me. "Best guests. Give them tea and toast, call it a continental breakfast, and they're good to go."

"Strange time of year for a sightseeing tour." I said. "Cold and hard to get out and about."

Danny laughed. "The seniors? You'd be surprised. Winter's different for them. A long time to be stuck alone in the house. A bus tour is a social event for that crowd. A chance to chat away, mile after mile. The secret to my success is that I can see opportunities where they lie." He searched for an example of this. "Take Iceland as an example. That place is packed. Wall-to-wall. And with a lousy name like that." He leaned in closer to share an insider's insight. "But if it was up to me, from a marketing perspective, I would change the name of that country. Rebrand it."

I didn't think the government of Iceland would take advice from Danny Dwyer, manager of the Anchor Motel, but I didn't say that. I had my own agenda.

"Danny, there's something I don't understand, and I think you are the person to help me."

The motel manager squared his shoulders and tried to look knowledgeable, which wasn't easy. "Shoot. Got a couple of minutes."

I started to speak but became distracted. I was at least five inches taller than Danny, and over his head, I spotted a new glass cabinet near the reception desk, with rusty articles of indeterminate identity arranged on its glass shelves.

"That new?" I asked.

"That there is a tourist attraction," Danny said proudly. "I got that cabinet at an estate sale. Someone else was after the china and crystal. That left me to take that fine piece of furniture off the family's hands. Got it for next to nothing."

I walked across the Anchor's worn carpet for a better look. Danny moved in close behind me, like a mother anxious that her child might touch or break something of value.

I studied Danny's display. The top shelf held a folded-over index card inscribed in flourishing cursive:

Historical artifacts found locally.

I examined the treasures. I recognized a few copper pennies, some of which looked like they had been deliberately flattened on some train tracks and left there for a winter. The sign next to them read:

SIMILAR TO THE FAMOUS NORSE
SILVER PENNY FOUND IN MAINE
(LESS THAN 500 MILES SW FROM HERE).

Next to the green pennies was a single old leather glove, stiff with age, three fingers chewed off, as if it had once been a dog toy. The card beside asked:

WASHED ASHORE FROM A SHIPWRECK?
THE *TITANIC*?

I stared at the motel manager. "Are you joking?"

"Only putting the question out there," Danny said, defensively. "It's up to people to make up their own minds." He studied me, searching for a diversion. "Hey, I got good deals on some new-to-you beach metal detectors behind the front desk. Interested?"

"Not a chance." Broken pottery on the next shelf caught my attention, and I leaned over for a closer look. "Where did you get those pieces of ceramic?" I asked. "They look familiar."

"You think?" Danny was enjoying himself. "I thought you would recognize your own merchandise, Val. Those bits and pieces are the seconds I found behind the pottery workshop downtown. The rejects. I guess some folks take time to get the hang of making pots."

I stood up and stared at the manager. "Those are leftovers from the mug-making class at the Co-op?" I knew I recognized the sea-green glaze, popular with tourists.

"Yup. I went through the recycling in the alley. Environmentally responsible. You know me."

I sure did. I straightened up and looked the motel manager in the eye. "Everything you've got here is a fake, Danny. You know that. Doesn't it bother you to misrepresent history? What did the Treasure Trovers think of this little display?"

"Some of them might have had a few words," Danny admitted. "But that's only because they're not entrepreneurs." He sniffed. "Can't make a living looking for loose change on a beach, can you?"

"Guess not," I said, "but I want to talk about a rock. One that was cut up to look like it had Viking letters on it. I think Percy thought it was authentic." I was careful what I said next. "I have it on good authority that this particular rock came from this property, dug up when you built the pool." I tapped on the glass of some lovely lady's ex-china cabinet, which had once held teacups and now housed found objects. "Does your entrepreneurial thinking involve the manufacture and distribution of big fakes to bring in tourists and treasure hunters? To attract attention?" I raised my hands in the air, either to express my exasperation or to get them in position in case shaking Danny became necessary.

A nice-looking couple of traveling retirees walked into the motel lobby, took one look at me, turned, and walked out.

Danny opened his mouth to defend himself, then narrowed his eyes and pressed his lips together.

"Harry Sutherland," he pronounced. "He's freelancing, isn't he? I knew I should never bring him in as a partner. An exclusive arrangement. Good for us both. He didn't tell me where he got his finds, and I didn't ask. Our mothers are friends. Harry was short of work, but he had the truck. I gave him a few dollars over the summer to haul away fill. When that was done, my mom asked me to see what else I could do. So, I told him if he had a plow for the front of the truck, he could do some clearing here come the winter." Danny laughed. "And look where that got me. Percy got himself stabbed. The RCMP was in my parking lot, worried my plow guy buried him, although it turned out there was no evidence of that. Lucky I didn't get charged with a health and safety violation."

Or murder, I thought. There was always that. "Look, Danny, what do you have to say about rocks with inscriptions from this property being deposited throughout the community?"

Danny crossed his arms. He looked past me at the two well-dressed seniors tentatively standing outside the motel's front door, trying to decide if they should check in or check out. "Harry swore up and down those boulders he found were the real deal," he said. "Look, maybe it was one of his that Percy saw. I have no idea. Go ask him and find out. That is, if you can find him. I never can."

Danny Dwyer might have found Harry elusive. I did not.

I called his mother.

"Harry is at the old church," Mrs. Sutherland said. "He's started to go there a lot. That's where his dad is, with all the other Sutherlands, at the old place on the north shore."

I knew the place. Toby and I often passed it on our walks. It was a peaceful and comforting place, the graves facing the waters over which the earliest residents had sailed from Scotland to Nova Scotia, their bones resting where they settled, their hearts looking back to the shores they left behind. The congregation worshiped in town these days, leaving the tiny church shut down, open only in the summer as a historical site.

It seemed a strange place for Harry to visit in the winter. If he was a regular churchgoer, it had not taken much effect. Was Harry really there visiting his dad? Sitting there on a bench between snowdrifts, looking out at the sea? Contemplating miracles? That wasn't the Harry I knew. It didn't feel right. Something else was taking him out to Shore Road in the middle of February. And whatever it was, I was certain of one thing.

Harry Sutherland was up to no good.

CHAPTER THIRTEEN

As I drove up to the churchyard where Harry's mother said I would find him, I passed the old fish plant. It was abandoned these days, left behind when the big corporate fishing operations started processing the catch onboard. Farther along the road, I passed the Bluenose Inn. I realized I hadn't seen Gareth since the day Percy disappeared and the knife was found. I also hadn't seen Simon or Rollie since I saw them constructing the chicken coop on the Inn's patio. The flock would be there now. I wondered how Catherine, and Dusty the cat, were handling the change. My cousin's partner was a stress baker. I could almost taste her lemon squares. Maybe I'd stop for a visit on my way back home.

A few miles past the Inn, the road bent, and the tiny church came into view. Harry's truck was parked beside it on a side road cleared only one car length. The church was small, a wooden structure with a narrow door at the front framed on either side with vertical windows, an arch at the top, and four lancet windows along the sides, one for each of the short rows of pews. It was a plain church, without a steeple, with a framed Heritage Trust of Nova Scotia crest mounted on the shingles. I pulled up and parked beside the snow-barricaded front door, got out, and followed the path a loyal former parishioner had undoubtedly snowplowed along the side of the building to the graveyard.

The route took me past a large old oil tank. Beyond it, I heard violent hammering. I kept walking. On the other side of the tank, I found Harry Sutherland bent over, attacking a granite headstone with a sledgehammer and heavy chains.

"Harry!" I yelled. "What are you doing? You don't desecrate headstones like that! Think of the family."

Harry stood up. He wore a dirty checkered work shirt, the heavy winter kind with a fleece lining inside. He had pushed safety glasses high up over his wool hat where they would do him no good and wore yellow leather work gloves at least two sizes too big on his hands.

"Geez, Valerie. You don't sneak up on a guy like that! Nearly gave me a heart attack."

I looked at the headstone. The name and most of the date after the dash was chipped away. "A heart attack?" I asked. "That would be what you deserve. What are you now? A grave robber? And your poor mother thinks you're visiting your dad."

At the mention of his mom, Harry did his best to snap back into reality.

"What are you talking about?" he asked with indignation. "I'm an artist. A craftsperson. Anybody should understand that, it would be you."

"Craft?" My voice was loud in the quiet snow. "Is that what you call smashing up headstones? What would your father think of that?"

"The old man would get it," Harry said, dropping his sledgehammer. "That man always made do with whatever he had to work with. He put a Weedwacker motor on a little rowboat once. I inherited his ingenuity." Harry's face cleared with understanding. "Ahh, I get it. You think I'm messing up *real* markers. What kind of a guy do you think I am? These are seconds." He held up a heavy chain. I recognized it from the store. It was a trucker's towing chain, used to make sure a load stayed secure. "I only do it to ones that got messed up at the headstone operation. I get them from my cousin. The one who doesn't spell so good."

"The guy who works at MacKay's Monuments?" I knew this cousin from school. Like Harry, he had majored in detention and trips to the principal's office. If there were two Sutherlands involved, it made sense that this project did not.

"That's the one," Harry said. "Earl. They started him in headstone polishing, but with inflation and everything, wage costs, global supply chain issues"—it was clear Harry had no idea what he was talking about—"they moved him into engraving the names. He messed this one up. He was going to dump it somewhere before the boss found out, but to help him out, 'cause he's family, I said, 'Dump it with me.'"

"What are you doing?" I asked. "Correcting his spelling?" I noticed other tools thrown down onto the icy gravel. "Hammer-and-chisel editing?"

Harry sighed. "No, Valerie. It's called distressing. Guys I know told me about it. They use chains to make old tables and dressers look older, for the tourists. The visitors love things all bashed up, paint missing." He paused to admire the distressing work he'd done on the battered rock on the ground, then continued. "Look around, all these old markers. The really old ones you can't read. No names, no nothing. The weather does it up here, the wind, sleet, salt air. I'm creative. Danny and me got this idea about making other kinds of markers."

I let this sink in. "Harry Sutherland, are you telling me you are up here, next to your own father's grave, manufacturing fake artifacts for a small-time motel operator who thinks this"—I pointed at the headstone and the chips of granite in the snow—"is going to turn Gasper's Cove into a World Heritage Site?"

"Maybe," Harry said. He tapped the edge of the granite block at his feet.

"This is the dumbest of all the very dumb ideas you have ever had. And why, in the middle of winter, did you drag that rock behind a church to work on it?" I asked. "Not very convenient."

Harry seemed surprised by the question. "Think about it. If a person's got something going on with a tombstone, where's the one place it's not going to stand out? A graveyard, am I right?" He looked over to the cleared grave, third row, second on the right. "Plus, working here, I'm near Dad. It's like quality time, you know? Him and me always did projects together." Harry's voice caught. I realized he was serious.

"There's one problem with your story," I said. "I talked to Danny. He told me he knew nothing about any rock monuments or what you were doing with them."

"Did he now? Slippery of him," Harry sniffed. "What he says is true, and it isn't. This is how it started. Danny got to telling me about how there was some talk a long time ago, around when they put in the causeway, about some Viking stuff. Nothing showed up. The talk died down, but then came the news about the old settlement they found in Newfoundland. Look at the tourist traffic it brought into a dull part of the region no one would go to even if they knew any better, Danny said. I thought he had a point. Then, Danny said he'd pay good money for anyone who found something like that here that was a real artifact. And bingo." Harry looked into the space above his head, as if he could see the lightbulb of inspiration there. "I thought of my cousin's problem with spelling. So, I made a—what do you call it? A prototype. Worked on it last summer before I got rid of it. I took a picture and sent it to Percy to ask what he thought."

"And Percy thought it was real?"

"I guess so," Harry said. "I do good work. And the picture was kind of blurry."

"Didn't he want to see the original?" Percy had taken the picture of Harry's fake to the meeting, and by coffee break he was gone.

"Of course he did. That's when I kind of panicked," Harry admitted. "A first edition is never a guy's best work, and I wanted to make some cash. Then, my cousin had another foul-up. He forgot to put the 'a' in MacDonald. I wanted to try again, make something that would hold up better when you looked close at it. That's why I'm working on this baby. It's turning out real good. I got rid of the beta version." Harry gave me a minute to be impressed with his command of technical language.

"That was the rock you dumped with Stuart?" I asked.

"You got it. It's harder to get rid of a headstone than you think. Putting it in the fill was perfect. I figured it would just end up under the sod in Stuart's front lawn." He shook his head. "How was I supposed to know Stuart would go all artsy on me and make it a feature?"

I wondered if Percy had been the only one who had seen the monument in Stuart's yard. "That rock has to go," I told Harry. "It's like a curse. I want you to go to Stuart's house, tell him what you told me, and remove it."

Harry laughed. "Good luck with that," he said. "If anyone says anything, I'll tell them it was a practical joke, and those aren't against the law. Don't forget, Valerie," Harry said, doing up the top button of his jacket, "it's winter. The ground's frozen solid like cement. There's no chance of moving that thing until the ground thaws. And that won't be for a couple of months."

"But Harry, something bad happened to Percy after he found your rock and started showing pictures of it around. And whoever did it is still out there. Maybe they know about this fake rune in Stuart's yard, maybe they don't. Maybe they don't care. I have no idea. It doesn't matter. The main thing is, your little project is sitting there like some sort of invitation in front of the house of a nice man and his teenage daughter. I've got to do something. I'm going to get the RCMP here. And if that gets you into trouble, you deserve it." I pulled out my phone and held it up to him. "I'm phoning Wade."

Behind me, I heard a car door slam, followed by the crunch of heavy boots on the ice and snow. Harry heard it, too, and looked past me.

"No need to make a call," he sighed. "Wade's right behind you."

CHAPTER FOURTEEN

And he was.

Officer Wade Corkum of the RCMP walked into view and stood between us.

He looked at the granite on the frozen gravel at Harry's feet, the tools, and the chips of stone in the snowbanks, then at me.

None of what he saw seemed to surprise Wade. I noticed his knitted tuque had been replaced by a muskrat hat, not as warm as it could have been, with all four flaps tied together on top of his head. Underneath it, he rolled his eyes.

"I don't want to know," he spoke to the snowbank. "I really don't."

This was not the reaction I expected. I carried on. "Glad you got here," I said, as if he had responded to a call I made. "Just in time. This here"—I knocked my boot against the edge of Harry's stone, slipped, and almost fell over. Harry reached over to help me, and being shorter than I was and only half my weight, we tottered a bit before I could stand up and continue—"is the evidence."

"Evidence of what?" Wade asked. He had the look of a person already halfway through a very bad day. "That you two most random operators are up to something, this time behind a church?" He looked hard at me. I could see my face in his mirrored aviator glasses. I needed to brush my hair. "And when I'm on the job, Valerie Rankin, it's RCMP Officer Corkum to you."

"Of course, Wade, I mean, Officer Corkum, slip of the tongue." I needed him to understand this was a serious, crime-reporting type of conversation. It had not gotten off to a good start. "You must be here for Harry. I can save you some trouble: I have his confession. He has been doctoring tombstone rejects—we can talk about where he got them later—to make tourist attractions for Danny at the motel. But one got turned into a lawn ornament in Stuart's yard. But we can't do anything about it until the ground thaws."

Wade slid his glasses down his many-times-broken-at-hockey nose and stared at us.

"But I would like ..." I decided to be more definite. "No, I *demand* that you give Stuart and his daughter police protection until Percy appears or his murderer gets caught." I was losing Wade's attention, I could tell. "Or until spring. Whatever comes first."

Wade blew out a big breath. The white cloud hung in the air between us before drifting away, dismissing me as it did. "I don't have one sweet clue what you are talking about here," he said, "and I am in the business of clues. And I'm not going to put any effort today in trying to make sense of what you just said. " He looked again at the distressed tombstone. "Whatever creative activity you have going on is not why I am here."

Harry's plaid shoulders sagged in relief. "What's going on, Officer Corkum?" he asked. This was the first time I had ever heard Harry call Wade anything but his first name.

"Snowplow," Wade said. "It's missing. And it's the only one on this island."

"Excuse me," Harry said, pointing to his truck with the short seasonal plow mounted on the front. "I've got mine right here."

"Not that." Wade was dismissive. "A real plow, the big one. The one the municipality sent over to do our roads. It's gone. I've been sent out to find it." The sunglasses were off and in a pocket. Wade studied Harry carefully. "Do you know anything about this?"

The fact that the municipal plow that competed with him for seasonal contracts was missing made Harry's day.

"Trying looking in the repair shop?" he snickered. "Institutional maintenance is not the same as loving care." He beamed at his truck, ignoring the cardboard and duct-tape repair work on the passenger-side rear window. "Drive local," he added, inspired.

Wade narrowed his eyes. He looked like a balding, middle-aged, ex-hockey star, an imitation of a fox about to outsmart and capture a pigeon. "If it snows, this would be good for you, wouldn't it, Harry? No other plow on the island until they can send one over?"

Harry was wary. "I suppose so," he said. "I always come through for the community."

"The community," Wade observed. "The same one who comes out to watch the hockey games at the arena. You've got some skill with that ice resurfacer, Harry. I've watched you spin around those corners of the rink. You know how to drive heavy equipment, I'll give you that."

Harry understood. His eyes did a quick sweep of the area. Those who might support him, me or his poor father, were quiet.

"I didn't take off with any municipal plow," he protested. "How would I do a thing like that, even if I wanted? Don't have no key."

This was an important point.

Wade wasn't done.

"Souvlaki?" Wade asked. "You like Greek food?"

Harry was relieved the conversation had pivoted away from snowplows. He leaned forward toward Wade. "Mom's a good cook," he shared. "But she's from around here. Lots of potatoes. *Lots.* Big on the hodgepodge in the summer, when the garden's in," he added, referring to a traditional Nova Scotia dish of green and wax beans, carrots, turnips, and potatoes, covered in water and boiled long and hard. "To Mom, salt and pepper are spices. But sometimes a man wants a little olive oil, a little garlic, some oregano." He stopped himself. "Don't tell her I said that," he pleaded to me.

Wade smiled. "Is that garlic I smell on you, Harry?" he asked. "From lunch? At the Agapi?"

Harry and I both wondered if this was a trick question.

"Oh, shoot," Harry said. "She'll know."

"What are you getting at, Officer Corkum?" I asked, rattled on Harry's behalf.

"The call came in from the Department of Transport about a missing unit lost over here," Wade said. "Nothing much on the roads at present, so a couple of the operators went to the Agapi for lunch. They saw you there, Harry. Having the house special."

"That a crime?" Harry asked. "Apart from the breath?"

"Nice jacket, there," Wade said as an answer, reaching over to swipe a snowflake from Harry's collar. He was enjoying this. I didn't know why. "Hang it up, did you? At the front, like everyone does? Next to the jackets from the Department of Transport guys?"

"Oh, hell," Harry said. "Never did it. Swear."

I was missing something. "Wade, Officer Corkum, what's this about?"

Wade didn't shift his gaze from Harry's now-moist face. "This is about the guy from Drummond who drives the Gasper's Cove plow, getting dropped off by his buddies at the look-off where the plow was parked. And finding both the plow and keys, which he swears were in his pocket when he hung his jacket up at the restaurant, gone."

"Aw, come on, Wade." Harry looked side to side. There was only one way out from behind the church, and the RCMP cruiser blocked it. "Where am I going to hide a full-size snowplow? On an island? Where everyone knows your mother? Get real. I got my own keys." Harry pulled a big ring of keys out of his pocket and shook them at Wade. "See these here? Mine. Only ones I got."

Wade put out his hand. "Give those to me," he said. "We'll leave your vehicle here. I'll send someone to get it. You're coming with me, Harry. Down to the detachment for a chat."

"We can be there all day and all night, but I'm not going to be able to tell you where that plow's at." Harry started to follow Wade, then stopped. "Because I don't know."

"That doesn't matter," Wade said. "We'll find it. We'll find it with or without you. All municipal vehicles are equipped with GPS. You should have thought of that."

After Harry and Wade left, I stood in the churchyard and felt sorry for myself. I had to talk to Wade, and he dismissed me. I needed advice. I needed someone to talk to. I needed Darlene.

I tried to text her, but all I got was a notification that the user had silenced messages. I checked the time. She was probably out. I hadn't heard from her for at least a day, and that felt strange, honeymoon or no honeymoon. I had assumed that when she married George, nothing would change. Maybe it had.

I stared at my phone, willing it, and Darlene, to wake up. Neither did, but I did notice another message, this one from Noah.

Got a minute?

What's going on?

I'm at the Inn. Can you come drop by?

Noah asked.

Sure. I'm on the Shore Road. Going there anyway. Why?

I found something about this Tristan guy Kay should know. I think it would be better if it came from you.

It never stops, I thought. It never stops.

CHAPTER FIFTEEN

By the time I arrived at the Inn, the sun had broken through the clouds. The hard crust of snow that had started to melt with a recent rain had frozen again, forming sequins that made the whole front lawn look like a giant sparkling wedding dress, carefully hand-stitched and beaded. Unlike the last time I had been here, the parking lot was full. I recognized Noah's car, Rollie's truck, and the SUV that Simon had rented to come up the coast.

Noah was on the front porch. I got out of the truck and made my way to meet him. Winter was the noisiest season of the year. With each step, my boots broke the ice into little shards of glass, crunching them underfoot like broken lightbulbs. Behind the Inn, I heard the surf hitting hard against the cliffs at the end of the property. Between the ocean and the building was a more muffled sound, a mutual cooing. Rollie was out on the patio, talking to his flock of chickens.

I held tight onto the railing as I climbed to the porch. Noah reached down a hand to steady me. I took it. Once on the indoor-outdoor carpeting next to him, bright green and put down for safety's sake, I hesitated. All bundled up in his parka, Noah looked serious, worried, and vulnerable. I wanted to ask him right away about Tristan. But to be polite, I thought I should ease into that conversation. Darlene had told me not to be an over-involved mother. I didn't want to reveal my true identity quite yet.

"What brought you out here today?" I asked.

"An animal-in-winter story," Noah shrugged. "How to keep them safe when the temperature drops. I figured I'd talk to Rollie and Catherine about their flock here. The cold's got to be hard on them. Chickens don't come with winter coats. Although," he added, chuckling, "I hear some of your crafters knit them bird sweaters." Noah was trying hard, but I could tell his mind was on other things.

"That's right," I said. "A couple of the ladies are in pretty deep with chicken-rescue organizations. You should talk to them."

Noah smiled. "I might do that, although Rollie and that guy Simon were very helpful. I got some shots of the two of them hovering over the hens, hand-feeding. They showed me the coop. It's packed tight with straw, and they're running out heat from the Inn."

"I don't know a lot about chickens," I admitted.

"Neither did until I arrived," Noah said. "Simon seems almost obsessed with their personalities. Do you know if there is no rooster in the flock, one of the hens takes over? She'll even crow in the morning. Do you believe that? Simon says the dominant hen in this bunch is the red one. He's quite taken with her. And apparently, if anything is threatening the flock, these alpha hens go out in front and sacrifice themselves to save the group." Noah laughed. "Who knew there was so much drama in poultry?"

"Not me," I answered. I had nothing to add about chickens, so I started first. "So, you've done some research on Tristan?" I asked, trying to sound indifferent. "Do you want to go inside where it's warmer? Or is this something you want to talk to me about out here?"

"It's not that cold," Noah said. "And this should stay between us, unless you decide you want to say something to Kay. I'll leave that up to you. And maybe don't tell her you heard this from me."

"Okay."

"Right." Noah put his hands into his pockets and looked at the horizon of the ocean. "First, you've got to remember I have a degree in journalism. I was taught that nothing could be published or broadcast without three sources to verify it was true. Baseline ethics." He stopped at the sound of heavy ice snapping free from bare tree branches, falling and shattering over the hard surface of the snow. "What I'm trying to say is, podcasters like Tristan don't always operate professionally. They share opinions like they're facts. Listeners often don't get that. And I have to say, it must be a lot easier to pretend you are a journalist when nobody is checking up on you."

"So, you decided to check out Tristan's work?"

"I did. I had a hunch, and I was right. The red flags were there."

I remembered the conversation from dinner. "You said something about harassing people he interviewed. Is that what you were talking about?"

"Yes. The families of some people he investigated accused him of invasion of privacy, of even stalking them. I dug deeper. I talked to a few people I know who work in that space. They said there was an unspoken agreement in the industry that you couldn't trust Tristan as a collaborator because he would steal the story for his show. But that's not the big one. There was some guy he'd exposed who claimed Tristan planted evidence on him. There were pages of old letters that this guy claimed he'd written years before that suddenly turned up in a drawer at the victim's place of work. The guy was a crook, no one believed him, and there was no way to verify his story, but he said Tristan set him up." Noah paused. "No one cared, and Tristan's podcast numbers took off."

"But all of this is a rumor, isn't it?" I asked. "How much of this has to do with Kay?" There was something else I felt I had to ask. "Are you being completely objective? You know, because of her?"

Noah's cheeks went red, and it wasn't just from wind chap. He paused and looked past me to the tree letting go of its icicles.

"I have a lot of respect for Kay," he said. "She could have opened a vet practice anywhere in the province, but she kept going with school. She wants to do the best she can. She's brave. So, yeah, the idea that somebody could take advantage of her burns me. And sure, that's one reason I checked Tristan out. But let's face it. Things have happened since he arrived. Like Percy. I'm a reporter. I'm going to follow up on anyone or anything that seems sketchy. I want to figure it out."

"Making any progress?" I asked.

"Not sure," Noah said. "Tristan says he's here on holiday, but there's talk in the community that he's nosy, walking around and asking a lot about the past. It feels to me like he's working on a story. I think he's following a lead. And I hate to say it, but the thing about being Kay's friend may be a cover. They haven't known each other that long." Noah stopped. "Sorry, maybe I shouldn't have said anything."

"No, I'm glad you told me." I remembered when Kay's dad and I had split up—the office rumors, the women. I had wished then that someone had warned me. "I don't want her hurt. Maybe we should both keep an eye on this Tristan. If we see something concrete, then we can tell her. Does that make sense?"

"It does," Noah said. "If I find out anything, I'll let you know, and maybe you do the same for me?"

The door of the Inn opened behind us. Catherine came out.

"Deal," I whispered.

"Is there a problem?" Catherine missed nothing, ever. "Why are you standing out in the cold? Come on in." As I passed her, Catherine gave me a look. "What were you two talking about?" she asked.

"Nothing. The chickens," I said, gesturing to the poultry residence on her side patio. "Let's have some tea, and you can tell me how that's going." I turned to Noah. "You coming?"

"Another time," he said. "I'm off. Got things to do. Valerie, good to talk to you. I'm glad we see this the same way." He smiled at Catherine. "I took pictures of your flock. I'll send the best shots to you. Maybe you can frame them."

Catherine rolled her eyes. "Not much of a chance of that," she said. "None at all."

After Noah left and Catherine had closed the big door behind him, she turned to me. "Okay, you weren't standing around out there in below-zero cold discussing poultry. What's going on?"

Not much got past Catherine.

"It's this friend Kay brought home," I explained. "Noah doesn't trust him. I'm not sure if he has good reason or if he's jealous."

"Hmm," Catherine said. "He did teach her how to surf last summer, didn't he?"

"He did, although I think she sees him primarily as a friend of her brothers' who hangs around the beach. Familiar. It's easy to overlook what's right there in front of you." I thought of the dinner. "She seems to enjoy Tristan's fancy food and talk about sponsors. Her life has been school and university."

"If she wants more glamour now, there's nothing you can do about it."

"You sound like Darlene," I said. The clucking from outside was getting louder. "What's it like living with chickens?" I asked.

"Basically, a mini version of human society. Gasper's Cove, but short, with feathers." She sighed. "And noisy. Like everyone else here. Some days, I miss being at the library. At least there, when I was stressed, I could go down and hide in the stacks, sit on one of the little stools, and think. In whatever section was most appropriate."

"What do you mean?"

"If I had a demanding patron, I'd go down to 155 and do some four-square breathing."

"155?" I asked.

"Developmental and differential psychology," Catherine explained, wistfully. "Always some answers there. Problems with municipal funding? 658, Management. Or maybe a detour to 352.1, Jurisdictional levels of administration. In my old library, that shelf was by the water fountain, so it was a good place to stop." Catherine sighed, heading toward the kitchen. "Now, I make tea for guests and fold towels. A lot of towels."

I followed her into the kitchen and saw she had a tray ready. "Who's that for?"

Catherine looked at the clock while she waited for water to boil. "Gareth. He'll be in the dining room now with a napkin on his lap."

I laughed and held the door open for Catherine and her tray of tea, scones, and gingersnaps. Gareth, as predicted, was waiting for her. While Catherine arranged her tea service in the dining room, I worked at information gathering.

"Professor," I began, "I've been thinking about you. There's been talk in town about Viking runes." I hoped this description was vague enough. I didn't want to go into Harry's fabrication experiments. "I've heard about the one in Yarmouth. What do you think of that one?"

Gareth grunted as he took his teacup from Catherine. "Hmm. Over the years, I've seen more than my share of these scams. All they do is consume the time of good academic researchers."

"Really?" I pressed on. "I know the stone in Yarmouth is questionable, but are there any other examples?"

Gareth picked up a napkin and wiped scone crumbs from his face. "Where do I start? Minnesota? Maine? Or here in

Canada?" He snickered. "The one they found in Ontario in the 1930s, they called the Beardmore relics. The claim was that they'd found a sword and a shield left by Vikings. As if those northern sea raiders ever bothered to make it to the farmland of central Canada. Planted, of course."

"Why would anyone make up a story like that?" I asked, although I had a good idea. There were those at the Anchor Motel who wanted to make us a World Heritage Site.

"Money, the most obvious." Disdain dripped from Gareth's voice. "Or attention. College students playing practical jokes. Or hope. Natural formations in glacial rock misinterpreted by the undereducated as evidence of pre-Columbian civilization. It takes a lot less time for rumor to spread than it does for rigorous scholars like myself to authenticate any finding. And in the meantime, of course, the site is contaminated."

I picked up a gingersnap and snapped it. I pretended to be a nice middle-aged woman making polite chitchat with an elderly man. "I understand you saw Percy's photo of something he found from around here." I tried to keep the interest out of my voice.

Gareth spread some of Catherine's excellent strawberry jam onto a scone and bit into it before he answered. "I'll be charitable," he said. "The photo on his little phone was poor, and I am a bit jaded when some amateur comes up to a meeting to show me something they think is the find of the century. My immediate impression was that what Percy had to show was a natural formation or some amateur's attempt at art. And our poor—and, I am afraid, late—friend, this Percy, seemed to be a gullible soul. One of the army of amateurs who spend their lives, as did the mediaeval alchemists, trying to find the philosophers' stone that would turn any base metal into gold. The problem, of course, is it doesn't exist, so they'll never find it."

"How did Percy handle it when you said the picture didn't look like anything important?" I asked.

"I never had a chance to tell him," Gareth said. "We went outside for a smoke, weak beings that we were, and I tried to think of how to phrase my impression in terms a man like him would understand. But before I could do that, he wandered off. I went inside, and that was the last anyone ever saw him, and my intention to be diplomatic seemed, if you pardon the pun, fairly academic."

"Was there anyone else there who seemed interested in Percy's picture?" I tried to keep the curiosity out of my voice.

Gareth stared at me. He was more interested in establishing his own identity than in noticing other people. "Not that I recall," he said.

Catherine took Gareth's cup and walked to the window. Rollie and Simon were still out with the hens. Gareth cleared his throat and looked at the old clock on the dining room wall, its hands clicking as loudly as they had for decades over the Roman numerals that marked their stately progression through time.

"Excuse me, dear ladies," Gareth said. "But I think it's time for my siesta. It's a habit I picked up on the digs when I was in South America." He grabbed his cane and heaved himself out of the burgundy damask upholstered chair with difficulty. Catherine turned from the window to help him. "Thank you, Madam," he said. "I'm off. A refreshed mind is a sharp mind. And who doesn't need that?"

CHAPTER SIXTEEN

I helped Catherine clear away the table, watching her sweep the crumbs off the embroidered tablecloth with a tiny silver dustpan and a little bristle brush. "Gareth has pretty strong opinions on amateur archeologists," I said as I loaded the tray.

Catherine shrugged.

"On that subject and everything else. That man needs twenty minutes to have a five-minute conversation. But to be fair, I think he's having a hard time with retirement. Lost authority. I guess lecturing is a habit that's hard to stop." She glanced at the windows, the heavy lace curtains held back in gold scrolls to let in the thin winter sun. "But to be honest, I'd rather be talked at by Gareth than interrogated by that other one."

I knew she meant Simon. I walked over to a window. Sure enough, Simon was out there, right behind Rollie, dictating into his phone, his jacket open, flannel shirt buttoned to his neck, corduroy pants hoisted, brand-new winter boots, laces untied, loose on his feet. There was duct tape over the bridge of his thick glasses. He looked harmless to me.

"At least the chickens keep him busy," I said. "And outside."

Catherine rolled her eyes. "Busy? It's like he's never seen a chicken before. He checks them every four minutes to see if they're laying. I think they've stopped just to annoy him." She pushed the dining-room door open with her hip, started to walk down the hall to the kitchen, and then stopped. She checked the Inn's reception area to make sure it was empty before she spoke.

"You know how Gareth was talking about fakes?" She hesitated and then continued. "I've got to share something with you. I haven't told Rollie this, and he won't like it when I do, but I've been doing some of my own bibliographic research." She reacted to the blank look on my face. "Titles. Books. I went deeper into Simon's publication history."

"You mean his young adult fantasy novels?" I asked. "The ones he wrote before he became a prepper?"

"Not those," Catherine waved away my question. "Have you heard of pen names?"

"I've heard of them, but I'm not sure if I know what they are. Aren't they like pseudonyms?"

"Sort of," Catherine said. "More accurately, pen names are something authors use when they want to change genres and they don't want to confuse the readers. For example, you might find a writer who will write romance novels under one name and dark thrillers under another."

"Are you telling me he has pen names?" I asked.

"That's exactly what I'm saying." Catherine waited until we were inside the kitchen to continue. She put down the tray on the big worktable in the middle of the room, pulled out two chairs, and sat down. She picked up the last gingersnap on the plate. "It turns out that this surviving-the-apocalypse book is not Simon's only work of nonfiction. Over the years, he has published other books that involved embedding himself in a situation and then writing about it."

The wind outside rattled the windows. My intuition whispered to me. I pushed the feeling aside and refocused on the conversation. "Like, undercover?"

"You got it," Catherine said. She leaned forward, as if to make sure that the next bombshell she dropped wouldn't shatter all over the table. "Listen to this: He spent two weeks on the Orkney Islands off the north coast of Scotland. Two weeks." Dusty, dozing on a dropped tea towel under a storage trolley, opened one green eye, the cat's version of being fully alert. Catherine continued. "And after that deep experience, he wrote something called *Life at the Edge of the World.* Another time, he worked at a restaurant in New York for a *weekend.* They fired him. Then, he wrote *Life in New York's Culinary Hell.* After a month of picking fruit on a farm down South? *Life's Not So Peachy in Georgia.* Do you know what I call this?" she asked.

"Being sneaky?" I suggested. "A poor guest?"

"He's that," she admitted, "but also something worse. Simon is here with innocent chickens and the love of my life under false pretensions. As a librarian, I'll tell you what he is." She raised a hand in the air for emphasis. "A cultural plagiarizer."

"A what?" I had no idea what Catherine meant, but this didn't sound good.

"He pretends to belong, but he doesn't. He's not here working on any prepper book. He came to worm his way into our lives so he can sell it. *Life in Pre-Contact Nova Scotia* or something worse. Purely 919: Geography of and travel in Australasia, Pacific Ocean Islands, Atlantic Ocean Islands, Arctic Islands, Antarctica, and on extraterrestrial worlds. I can see it. We're one more thing he can market."

"But why make a fuss about the cold-weather survivalist stuff? He seems to be genuinely interested in that," I protested.

"Of course he is. That's an angle. Life on this island has never been easy. But we're not reality TV. It's who we are." Catherine was grim. "The pumping Rollie for information has to stop."

"What are you going to do?" I asked.

"Let him know I have him figured out. I have a life here to protect," she said, crossing her arms over her Fair Isle sweater. "I gave up a secure, public-service job, with an excellent pension and benefits, in my mid-forties, to come here and scrub out bathrooms and wash sheets with Rollie Rankin. Everybody thought I was crazy. I was on track to be the head of interlibrary loans for the whole system. I know my colleagues thought I was a desperate spinster making a mistake."

"No one thought that at all," I said, although that was probably exactly what they thought.

Catherine's cheeks had bright pink spots in the middle of them. "I never married. Anyone who might have asked worked with me, and I didn't want to live with another version of myself." Catherine looked at the rings on her fingers. Rollie had given her three. "Promise" rings, he called them. I assumed one day, he'd smarten up and spring for a diamond.

"Don't laugh," she said. "I didn't just go into the stacks when I wanted advice. Sometimes, when I worked the late shift, I'd visit 813.085: Romance fiction." There was a faraway look in her eyes. "On one of those nights, I was having a browse, and I looked up. And there was this huge man, with a big red beard and clear blue eyes. I felt he could see right into who I was. It was like he stepped out of a book. To appear like that, in the 800s section. Well, I knew it was a sign."

I gave Catherine a moment to relive her memory. "A sign? What happened next?" I asked.

Catherine pulled herself back to the present. "I'll never forget that night. He asked me where he could find books on running a bed-and-breakfast. The words I said next changed my life."

This was beautiful. "They were?" I asked. I held my breath.

"The call number. 647.94: Lodging for temporary residents; bed-and-breakfasts, hotels, hostels, inns, motels, resorts. And here we are." She looked around the kitchen of the old sea captain's mansion and then at me. "You don't borrow someone else's life. You write your own."

As I drove away from the Inn, I thought of what Catherine had said and, for some reason, of Stuart. The snow swirled in my headlights, and I struggled to keep in my lane, with all sight of the center lines gone. I hoped Stuart and Erin were home, safe and warm. I turned on the radio.

Well, folks, here we go again. Listeners have been calling in to tell us about the Environment Canada weather app, which is calling for blizzard-like conditions. Folks, like we always say here, the real news is local, and so is the weather. Information from our own weather station is that any flurries will move right past us and out to sea, like they almost always do. And one gentleman caller pointed out, lots of these apps are full of misinformation. Nothing outside your window we haven't seen before. This, too, shall pass.

I turned the radio off. I crouched down in my seat to see the road, as best I could, through the arcs made by the windshield wipers. Really, CKGC? No blizzard? Are you sure?

I'd lived in this climate my whole life. I knew what I was seeing. I'd walked back and forth to school in all sorts of weather growing up. I could read the weather as well as anyone. There were three kinds of snow. The first was snow for show. That one was decorative and fluffy, pretty to look at, but quick to melt when it hit the ground.

The next type was the standard snow that was compact and purposeful, that fell not in flakes so much as economy-brand pellets, that fell and organized itself into stiff drifts.

And then there was snow like this tonight. Go-straight-home snow, no stopping. Snow that could cover Percy Skinner, wherever he was. This was snow that felt like frozen sandpaper on cheeks, that went over the top of boots and down inside to make balls on woolen socks. It was snow that made mothers watch at the windows in the fading light and wait, scanning the horizon for the smaller children trailing behind siblings, stepping into the holes made by bigger boots.

This was long-term snow. Snow with its own agenda.

Mean snow.

Hard and dangerous.
Why hadn't anyone warned us?

CHAPTER SEVENTEEN

I wondered if I would make it.

I cursed the plow that hadn't cleared my way; then, I remembered there wasn't any plow. It was gone. Like Percy. The road had disappeared too. I had no way of knowing if I was driving in the right lane, the visibility was that bad. I fought with the wheel to move me back to where I thought I should be, and I thought of Toby waiting at home. The snow kept coming down, and that gave me some traction. Finally, I made it off the Shore Road and saw the lights of Gasper's Cove. I was almost home. I was exhausted.

The snow on my street was thick; the community mailbox on the corner was half buried in drifts, and the street sign was covered in a dense pillowcase. End-to-end, side-to-side, the whole street was a flat, white blanket, as if the built features—road, curbs, sidewalks, walkways, and driveways—underneath the snow didn't exist. Here and there, I saw mini tornados and a few headlights, pulsing along driveways. Some of my neighbors, the retired men, were out with their snowblowers, attempting with their five horsepowers to take on a northern storm that had the power to go all the way up the coast of Nova Scotia, across the Cabot Strait, across to Newfoundland, and as far as Labrador if it wanted, and would erase their efforts by morning. Snowblowing in a snowstorm, wives inside warm living rooms shaking their heads.

I had left my front steps light on. I could see Toby was at the window, waiting for me. I approximated my driveway, turned in, and hoped I wasn't churning up my front-yard rhubarb when I parked.

My door jammed when I tried to push it open against the snow. Who would take a snowplow in a storm? What would anyone but a municipally paid operator even know what to do with it? A plow was a very specific piece of equipment. If it wasn't being used to clear all of this, what was it being used for?

I trudged through the thigh-high waves of white to my front door. I located the steps with the feel of my boots because I couldn't see them, found the doorknob, and pushed. A ledge of snow fell into the house, and Toby slid on it on his way out, past me and down the steps. Business done, he turned and struggled back up the stairs, until he was beside me.

"I'm so sorry," I said, bending down to hug the dog and shepherding him back inside. There would be no dog walking tonight. "Mommy has had a busy day. Let's get supper." I shrugged off my coat, threw it into the hall closet, kicked off my boots, and dropped my bag on a chair. I reached into it and pulled out my phone. I'd missed a call from Stuart.

He picked up on the first ring.

"Where have you been? I was worried." I heard Birdie and Erin horsing around in the background.

"I was up on the Shore Road," I said. "I had a chat with Harry behind a church. Then, I dropped by the Inn to see Catherine." I remembered Stuart had Municipal Public Works connections. "Did you know they lost the snowplow?" I wanted to laugh. After the tension of the drive home, the idea no one could find something that large struck me as funny.

"I did, it's insane." The background sound of barking faded. I picked up a muffled "Take that dog and that sock into the other room, please. I'm talking to Val." Erin responded with something she seemed to think was hilarious, and then Stuart was back. "That's one reason I was worried," he continued. "How were the roads?"

"Terrible and getting worse," I replied. I left out my adventure in the oncoming lane. I stuck my nose on the cold glass of the front door. The fir trees on either side of the steps were now covered almost to the top. The indentations my boots had made only moments ago in the drifts had disappeared. "I thought this storm was supposed to go out to sea."

"It hasn't, has it?" Stuart agreed. "Environment Canada has revised it to a severe storm warning, and with the plow AWOL, the local guys can't get out to the weather station on the island."

"I don't think we need experts," I said. "This is more of a look-out-the-window situation. We're going to be snowed in for sure." The thought didn't upset me. Like all Canadians, I was genetically predisposed to prepare for storms. Here at home, I knew I would have lots to eat, and if the power went out, Toby and I could fire up the wood stove in the basement. There was no point in living in a tiny community clinging to the rocky shore of the North Atlantic if you weren't ready for emergencies.

Stuart thought the same way. "Wood?" he asked.

"Lots."

"Gas in the car?"

"Half a tank. And antifreeze in the wipers."

"Good. Keep your phone charged," he added, as if ticking off some invisible list in his head. It occurred to me that Stuart, not Simon, should be writing the survivalist's handbook.

"I will, but I have a landline, too, remember?" I looked at the beige rotary wall phone on the wall beside the fridge. Many houses in Gasper's Cove still had them.

"Right. Smart to keep it." Stuart sounded distracted. "Hang on, a message from the province. Give me a sec."

I walked into the kitchen and picked up Toby's bowl. I opened a cupboard with one hand while I waited for Stuart.

"Oh, hell," he said. "I was worried this would happen."

"Worried about what?" I asked.

"I'll read you the advisory," he said. "Here goes."

The Gasper's Causeway, which connects the community of Gasper's Cove to the town of Drummond on the mainland, will be closed today at 5:00 p.m. until further notice due to severe whiteout conditions and a high storm surge.

I knew what this meant. The snow wasn't our biggest problem: Changes in atmospheric pressure could send giant waves onto the causeway. I'd seen it happen before, land and sea disappearing into each other, blending into one black environment. No one could cross the causeway during a storm surge, not safely.

Stuart kept reading.

As the storm system continues to bring severe winter weather and whiteout conditions across Nova Scotia, drivers are warned to keep off roads for the safety of themselves and others, as travel is extremely difficult. No route onto or off Gasper's Island is available at this time, by land or by sea.

"Sounds bad," I said. The causeway was our lifeline to the rest of the province. Things had to be bad for Public Works to shut it down.

"It is," Stuart said. "Some poor guy in a tractor trailer already flipped over the side. They say it caused wicked damage to the infrastructure." I heard water running. Stuart must be filling the kettle for tea. I walked over to the counter and did the same. "I was afraid of this."

"What do you mean?"

"I did an assessment a while back. The causeway is like an iceberg; the important stuff is below the surface, settled right into the ocean floor. Every time we have a massive storm like this one, the erosion is accelerated, and more of the armor rock underneath is lost."

"What's armor rock?" I asked.

"The big rocks that support and protect the causeway," Stuart explained. "We've been losing them for quite a while now. When they go, there's nothing to stop parts of the causeway from slipping away back into the ocean. Incredibly dangerous."

"And we would be cut off?" I asked.

"You got it," Stuart said. "There would still be boats, and they might get something like the old ferry going again when the water calms down. But you're right. If the causeway collapsed completely, it could be months, even longer, before you could drive off the island. I warned them. My report argued that remediation was overdue. I told them not to wait for it."

"Wait for what?" I asked.

"The storm of the century."

CHAPTER EIGHTEEN

I heard Stuart's kettle whistle in his kitchen in Drummond. I walked over and took my own kettle off the stove. Even when our conversation ended, I felt we were still connected, simultaneously drinking our tea in our respective kitchens.

I hadn't told Stuart, but the idea of being cut off from the mainland didn't upset me. Not one bit. People like me saw being forced to be at home as more of an opportunity than a hardship. The less the outer world wanted us, the more time and space there was for our projects. I sometimes wondered if there would be any Gasper's Cove crafters without winter. November to April marked our creative season, when we turned gray into color, cold into warmth, and isolation into fellowship. To us, a storm day could be a gift.

I was going to enjoy mine.

I went downstairs to my sewing room in the basement and turned on the light. I eyed the potbelly wood stove in the corner, vented to the outside through what had once been a small, horizontal basement window. Stuart had stacked logs against one of the walls, like puzzle pieces, in an almost mathematical arrangement. He said he'd bought too much for himself and hadn't wanted to waste it. I doubted if this was true.

I had LED lights for my sewing table, bought to reduce the clutter of cords and to avoid having a power bar on my work area. The sticker on the lights said that if the big power went out, they would still let me knit or do my hand-sewing for at least sixteen hours. In another corner, the one farthest away from the wood stove, was my big chest freezer. In an emergency, if the power went out, I knew as long as I kept the lid down, the food in there would last for a good two days. And as backup, next to the freezer were the shelves of canning I'd done over the summer—no moose meat or fish (that would be in other basements along the street) but tomatoes, peaches, pears, beans, beets, jars of chicken broth, bread-and-butter pickles, chowchow, crab-apple jelly and strawberry jam, and even more in the basement at the store. Upstairs, I had stockpiles of crackers, canned milk, and tins of beans. Under the stairs, gathering dust, were four big eighteen-liter jugs of water. I was ready for anything.

Secure and snug, I threaded up my machine. I pulled out the pair of jeans Kay wanted me to hem. Like sewers anywhere, I would rather sew something new than do alterations and repairs, but I made an exception for family. Kay was tall, about 5 foot 7, 2 inches shorter than I was, and I often shortened her jeans when she was home. I couldn't believe the price she paid at the tailor's. So far, I had already unpicked the hem, trimmed it, and basted it up. I was at the ironing board, using the iron and my hardwood tailor's clapper to flatten the seams, ready to topstitch, when a message from Darlene flashed on my phone.

Why didn't you tell me?

Tell you what?

I tapped back.

Percy. What happened? Who did it?

I lifted the iron, sat it upright, and turned it off.

No idea what you're talking about.
Percy?

I swiped my thumb and found *The Lighthouse Online* newsfeed:

> BREAKING—Jacket of missing and believed injured man found ashore. Foul play suspected. Search for body postponed until after the storm. Updates to follow …

Reading.

My fingers hovered over the tiny screen. I didn't have any answers for Darlene. But I had a thousand questions of my own.

Foul play?

I wrote.

How do they know that?

Come on. There was a knife, blood, and his clothes on the beach.

I waited. I knew Darlene would have more to say.

What do you think happened? That he knifed himself, left his car, walked half a mile to the water and threw himself into the ocean?

Good point.

I answered her. Who could I call to find out more? I had a feeling Wade wouldn't tell me anything.

Who found the jacket?

I asked. That would be a good place to start.

Where have you been? Why do you think we texted you? It was Kay's friend who found it. Near the look-off on Shore Road. Down on the rocks. The RCMP changed Percy's status from missing to presumed dead.

I dropped my phone onto the ironing board, and it slid down onto the floor. I picked it up.

Going to call her. Will let you know.

I signed off, too overloaded to add the heart emoji.

I sat down in my sewing chair and tried to think. I knew that stretch of the coast. The look-off was above it, halfway between the Inn and the church where I'd found Harry. The rocks on that beach were large and jagged, and this time of year would be covered with ice. No one would have a reason to go there or want to.

So, why had Tristan?

I called three times before Kay answered her phone.

"Kay, it's me. Mom. I heard about Percy and the jacket. What happened?"

"Oh. Mom. Don't worry. It was yesterday, early. Tristan wanted to see the water in a storm surge, so he went to the coast. That's where he found this jacket, all wet. He's a curious guy—I mean, look at what he does—so he picked it up. He's seen a lot, so he thought it wouldn't hurt to drop it off with the RCMP. Just in case, you know?"

I didn't know. It wasn't as if the RCMP had a jacket lost-and-found department. This story didn't add up.

"Where's Tristan now?" I asked.

"No idea," Kay said. "He's gone out again. I don't think he understands our weather. He doesn't have the right boots for it. I hope he doesn't get lost."

"How long has he been gone?"

"About two hours. When he heard the jacket he found belonged to Percy, he said he had another hunch to check out. In a blizzard. I'm worried about him."

"Does he have his phone with him? Did you call?" I asked.

"That's the thing," Kay said. "He took all his gear and his mic with him. I have a feeling he is recording for his show. That would be why he's not answering. He turns everything off when he's working on the podcast."

"Well, there you go," I said. "Give him time. And call me back if you don't hear from him soon." I hesitated. Noah's information about Tristan weighed heavily on me. I had to ask. "This thing he's working on—was it something that he thought about before he came here, or something that came up? He seems to be talking to a lot of people. "

I had hit a nerve. "Mom," Kay said sternly, as if she were the mother and I were the child, "you don't understand the kind of work someone like Tristan does. I understand Tristan's work. He looks for story ideas everywhere he goes. That's why he's so good at what he does."

I tried to smooth things over. "OK, I understand. But, just out of interest, where did he go?"

"The causeway, I think. To see why it's closed. It's news, rocks fallen over the side," Kay said. "He's in the news business, so he probably wanted to check it out."

I looked over to the basement windows. They were already completely covered with snow, like some kind of white curtain hanging outside the window. Whatever Tristan wanted to see, I doubted if he could see much. There was meowing in the background.

"Mom, got to go, it's 5:00. Dinner time for the cats. Talk to you later."

"Love you," I said. But Kay hung up before she heard me.

I pushed my phone to the back of my table. It was my dog's dinner time too. I looked at the patient dog at my feet, his head close to the foot control of the machine. I clipped my last thread and put my scissors down. Toby stood up and banged his head on the underside of the table.

I smoothed my hand over the top of my dog's head, feeling the ridge of bone under his fur, covering a brain that held no troubles, only thoughts of his family, home, food, walks, and the sneakiness of cats. Dogs have shorter lives than we do, their days extended by joy and innocence. We went upstairs. I opened the back door. When I let Toby out, a wall of snow pressed up against the house, as if waiting to get in, collapsed onto the linoleum. Toby stepped over it and made his way out onto the deck. In weather like this, it was the best we could do. There would be no walks tonight. He understood that.

A few minutes later, he was back outside the door. I let him in, and he shook balls of snow across the kitchen floor. I got out an old towel and cleaned them up before they melted. It was cold. We were both hungry. I filled Toby's bowl, opened the fridge, and pulled out leftover chicken and vegetables to reheat for myself. After the dishes were done, Toby followed me into the living room and lay down by my comfy chair. He knew our evening routine. I had one more look at the storm, picked up my knitting, and joined him.

I worked on a pair of socks for Paul in New York. I'd just finished a pair for his girlfriend, in earthy colors I felt were stylistically consistent with the eggplant tattoo on her elbow. I wondered if the elusive Tristan was the hand-knitted-sock type. I had only seen him in head-to-toe black. I didn't feel excited about knitting black socks. On the other hand, blue ones with surf waves would be fun to do. I caught myself. I had promised Darlene I would mind my own business.

As I worked my way back and forth across the heel, I thought about Percy. What no one said, we were all thinking: Percy had been attacked outside the motel and transported elsewhere, dead or, worse, dying. Thrown into the ocean. No one could survive outside long, and certainly not in the water.

I turned on the light so I could count my stitches and felt the darkness trapped on the other side of the window watching me. I did my decreases for the toe, grafted it closed, stood up, and stretched. Toby padded along behind me when

I walked down the hall to the bathroom. I turned on the tap in the bathtub and tested the water. It was icy. I waited until it ran hot, then put in the plug. With the dog still with me, I went down to the bedroom, opened a drawer, and pulled out plaid pajamas as soft and as thick as the flannel sheets on my bed. On the way back up the hall, I stood and looked out to see the stars like sparks in the sky. The moon, nearly full, and bright, reached down and joined hands with the snow, as if they could cup the horizon where we temporary settlers lived. The land, the sea, and the sky were seamless on winter nights like this and never this joined any other time of year.

The wind couldn't come inside, but the deep stillness could. The silence spoke to me, but I couldn't hear what it was trying to say. I looked out into the winter night and wondered what answers it had for me, or if it saw things I could not.

I turned away from the window and went down to turn off the tap in the bathroom. I was safe inside, the cold locked out. The wind howled but couldn't get in. I turned on the hallway light. The darkness could stay on the other side of the window until tomorrow.

CHAPTER NINETEEN

The next morning, the rumble of my phone on the bedside table woke me up. I sat up in bed, carefully, so I wouldn't wake Toby.

Darlene.

Are you alright? We saw the video. Too early to call our parents. Thought we'd ask you.

I reached over and turned on the light beside the bed. The house was warm, the heat pump whirring.

What video?

So far, Darlene's Cuban honeymoon had included a lot of checking in with Gasper's Cove.

We watched YouTube. Big emergency. People could die. We're worried.

What? Take it easy.

I tapped back.

No one is going to die. We had storms like this all the time when we were kids. What do you mean, YouTube?

I pictured George and Darlene looking at the snow in Gasper's Cove on a tiny screen, oblivious to the sun outside. I hoped they got a good deal on that all-inclusive package.

"The Eye of the Storm." One million hits. You've got that famous storm chaser there. He did one segment standing in front of the restaurant, up to his waist in snow. George had a fit.

Relax.

My phone dinged again. Stuart. It wasn't even seven o'clock. Toby shifted position.

Let me look at the YouTube thing. They'll get us dug out, and I will go around and see everyone's parents. It's all good.

I almost added that the roads would be cleared as soon as the missing snowplow was recovered—surely, Wade could find it—but reconsidered. That was a long story, and Darlene needed to get back to her honeymooning.

Thank you. Talk soon. ❤

I glanced at Stuart's message.

Call me.

I'd do that, but not before I saw the video that had Darlene and George so worked up.

I knew YouTube well. It was a great place for finding knitting fixes. The more I knit in the evenings, the more useful those were. I went back and read Darlene's message to get the name right and typed in "Eye of the Storm."

The ads on the screen woke up Toby.

When the advertising was finally over, Jason Black appeared. The face on the screen was more animated than the one I had seen in the hallway of the Anchor Motel. Dressed like a turn-of-the-century explorer, flaps of his fur hat flapping, wrap-around ski sunglasses hiding his eyes, Jason and his handheld video recorder rocked in the wind.

> *Jason Black, Extreme Weather Storm chaser here with an exclusive from Gasper's Cove, Nova Scotia, Canada, a community in crisis. Citizens here are in life-threatening situations. Cut off from all help. No one, not even life-saving services, can get in or out. The people here have been hit by a freak blizzard of a magnitude no one could have predicted. Environment Canada warned there was a storm coming, but no one, I repeat no one, could have anticipated the scale that has completely disabled this devastated community. But as a meteorologist, I listened to my instincts, and I deployed here a few days ago. It appears I am the only storm chaser embedded in the eye of this storm. But whatever the risk, I will post updates from this lonely and remote community that may find itself cut off from the rest of the world for the last time. Signing off for now. The responsible thing for me to do is to join in the search for signs of life on this desolate island, but I will keep you all informed with my on-the-ground reports during this extreme, extreme weather event. Wish me luck. Stay safe.*

I rolled my eyes. Darlene and I had walked home from school in worse weather than this. In those days, many mothers didn't drive, and if they did, they would assume that perfectly healthy Nova Scotia children could handle whatever nature doled out.

I dialed Stuart.

He didn't even say hello. "I'm on my way over," he said.

"How?" I asked. "Have they opened the causeway?"

"Nope, not yet," Stuart said. "But the old fishermen have their boats out, ready to transport anyone in an emergency, like they did in the old days. They know the Strait and that water. Bad weather never stopped them."

"You're getting them to bring you over?" I asked. "Why?"

"A couple of reasons," Stuart said. "I want to get a closer look at the causeway. I need to see what kind of damage has been done. I'm the guy who did the last inspection. After I've looked at that, I'm going to get the boat to take me all the way over. There's something else I want to check. And a few people I want to check in on." Stuart paused. I didn't say anything. I expected the trip would include a stop at my front door. "Harry's meeting me at the wharf with his truck. He's meeting the boats like a taxi."

"Got it," I said. Out the window, I saw the snowblower brigade at work clearing the new snow from the street, fanning out like an advancing army of elderly men with large, bought-on-special snowblowers. These units sprayed dramatic fountains of snow high up in the air, building walls of snow on either side of the street. Here and there, I saw mugs propped up in the snowbanks. I doubted all of them contained coffee. "Have they found the plow?" I asked. "We sure could use it over here."

"No," Stuart said. "That's the thing. I talked to Wade. He says they know someone lifted the keys and made off with it, but they still don't know why or what happened. Teenagers is the working theory, but that's what they always say. Wade thinks it's something more intentional."

"Intentional?"

"Yup. Most people don't know this, but all snowplows are outfitted with GPS. The town wants to keep track of which streets are cleared and which aren't. Locating it shouldn't be a problem. But it is."

"Why?"

"The GPS on that unit isn't showing up. That could mean one of two things. First, that the plow was wrecked—like, driven off a cliff. Dangerous and not easy to do. Hard to imagine no one noticing that, even in storm conditions."

"That's one theory. What's the other idea?"

"That whoever took it knew what they were doing and disabled the GPS," Stuart said. "I don't think there's many people over there on the island who know enough to do that."

Or many in Drummond either, I thought but didn't say. "Very weird," I observed. "It's one thing to do a prank. Another to steal something that big, and obvious, on purpose." Some little idea at the back of my brain raised its hand and pushed its way to the front of the crowded lineup in my mind. I remembered something I'd heard recently.

"Jason Black," I said, snapping the two words together like fingers. "YouTube. The 'Eye of the Storm.'" I remembered the stream of ads leading into his clip. "He's the one person who will make money if he is the only one reporting from the center of this 'storm of the century.' The longer we're holed up here, the better he'll do." I jumped out of bed, scuffed on my slippers, and headed down the hall, one arm in my housecoat. Toby followed me, tail wagging for no reason except that I was active. "Stuart. Jason Black took the plow. It had to be him."

"It had to be someone," Stuart agreed. "And it wouldn't make sense for it to be a local. You might have something there. I'll mention it to Wade. I think he's already over on the island." In the background, I heard Stuart's daughter asking her dad a question. "Look. I've got to get Erin and the dog next door so I can get the boat. Harry's meeting me on the other side to take me up to the look-off. He says he can get through with his truck."

"The look-off?" I asked. "Not going to be much of a view in this weather."

"Not going for the view," Stuart said. "There's something bothering me. It's the readings from the weather station up there. They don't jive with any other data in this area. I want to get in and take pictures to send to a couple of friends at Environment Canada. See what they think. It's bothering me that if we'd taken this storm more seriously, we'd have been better prepared. Maybe we should have closed the causeway earlier, as a precaution. That would have kept that truck that spun out off it. We're lucky that the driver wasn't hurt. He could have been. There's a lot of blame to go around. Some of it should come to me. I'm kicking myself that when the weather started to turn, I didn't go out and check those anchor rocks and make sure they were secure."

"I'm sure you did your best with the information you had at the time," I tried to reassure him. Stuart grunted. My attention wandered. I could see it now. The look-off. The weather hut. The last time I was there. High above a beach where Percy Skinner had been so many times, waving his metal detector back and forth over the sand and the rocks. Where his jacket had been found.

Yes, the look-off. Where I'd stopped, and a truck had swerved past me. One with a peach on the license plate, from Georgia. Jason Black's home state. He'd said it on YouTube: He was trained as a meteorologist. Someone who would know how to mess with the instruments and alter the readings at a tiny out-of-the-way weather station. Someone who could have kept an impending blizzard under the literal radar, to keep other storm chasers away.

The Anchor Motel. My mind raced to the next connection. Jason was there the night Percy was hurt and disappeared. What had Percy done? Had he told Jason he'd seen him up at the look-off? A witness could lead the RCMP to consider Jason's motive and then his crime. Exposure like that, as a fraud, wouldn't do much for the storm chaser's danger-man reputation or his career. If he'd stolen and stowed the plow, what would be his next move? If it were me, I would go back to the weather station and cover my tracks before anyone figured out I'd tampered with the readings. If he'd killed Percy as a witness—and I was sure I was right about that—what would he do to someone who found him at the scene of another crime?

My hand tightened on my phone. "Don't you and Harry go up there! Stay away from the look-off and Jason if you see him. He killed Percy. Stuart? Do you hear me?"

I looked at the tiny screen. My call to Stuart had dropped. The storm had taken him out of range.

What was I going to do? I ran to the front window. The snowblowing seniors were only halfway to the end of the street. Even if I dug out my truck, I couldn't go anywhere. I was trapped. I turned on the radio. CKGC said all roads were closed and to stay at home until further notice. They gave an emergency number, which I recognized was for the RCMP detachment in Drummond. I called it and asked to speak to Officer Corkum.

The officer at the desk slowed me down with her questions.

"Is this a medical emergency?" she asked.

"No, but ..."

"Are you stranded?"

"I'm home, safe in my house."

"Are you reporting a crime?"

"Yes." Finally. "A murder, a snowplow theft, and possible violence at the weather hut up on the look-off."

There was a pause at the other end of the line.

"Is this Valerie Rankin?"

"How did you know?" I asked. I was in my kitchen now, using the landline, no caller ID.

"Lucky guess," the officer said, "and it's that kind of day."

"I need to speak to Officer Corkum," I insisted. "It's urgent." I knew this woman from past encounters. She was of the if-we-do-it-for-you-we'll-have-to-do-it-for everyone school of public communication.

"Look, Ms. Rankin. Don't know if you've noticed, but we've got a weather event going on. Lots to deal with. Officer Corkum is unavailable. Can I take a message?" I thought her sigh was unprofessional.

I was not going to let her get to me. "Yes. And promise you'll give it to him. I've known Wade since high school." I was a little ashamed of myself for pulling relationship rank on the desk officer, but this was a crisis situation.

"You and half of Gasper's Cove and Drummond. The rest used to play hockey with him." The officer was unimpressed. "You said there was a message? Can I have it? I have a call on the other line."

"Tell him, immediately, that the person who killed Percy Skinner is a YouTube weather guy by the name of Jason Black. And if Stuart and Harry are already at the look-off, he might kill them too." I stopped to breathe. It was hard. My chest was tight with fear. "Wade has to save them," I pleaded, "and arrest Black."

"Slow down," the officer said. "Let's see if I got this right. There are two people who might be on their way to the look-off on Gasper's Cove in the middle of the worst storm in years. They are Stuart Campbell, the engineer, and Harry Sutherland, the Harry Sutherland. And you feel a third person, someone from YouTube, could show up there and cause an altercation? Did I miss anything?"

"Not really. If Harry can get Stuart up to the look-off in his truck, Black could get there, too, particularly if he's still got that snowplow he stole."

"Right," the officer sounded weary. "The message is, Officer Corkum is to go to the look-off to stop an argument between people who might not even be there in this storm, one of them possibly driving a stolen snowplow? Got it. Goodbye, Ms. Rankin."

And that was it.

I stood in my unrenovated kitchen and listened to the old-fashioned dial tone in the receiver of the old-fashioned phone on my wall and despaired. I opened a cupboard and poured out a handful of chocolate chips. I had failed to save Stuart. I doubted Wade would get my message in time. Who was Jason Black? What kind of career was storm chasing, anyway? How unstable must a person be to deliberately go right into the middle of a blizzard when they could be inside, visiting with family, or maybe knitting? It wasn't normal to live like he did. But normal people didn't kill, did they?

I tried Stuart's number again, first on the wall phone and then on my cell. The screen there told me that the number was still unavailable. I tried Harry and got the same message. I sank to the kitchen floor, put my arms around Toby, and tried to think. The dog leaned into me in solidarity and to listen.

"What am I going to do?" I asked him. "Even if I shoveled out the truck, I couldn't get there. Not on these roads."

Toby went still.

I'd said the word *truck*. Like *car*, it was one of his favorites. It meant walks on the beach, visits to Rollie, and treats.

Of course. A solution. I hugged Toby.

The last time we were there, his tail had knocked over a display of Catherine's brochures. I'd helped her pick them up. One was called *Things to Do in the Area*. Number one was the look off, with its "panoramic view of the Atlantic Ocean. Just a short walk."

I stood up, went over to the phone on the wall, and called the Inn.

Catherine answered.

CHAPTER TWENTY

"Valerie," Catherine said, "how are things in town? You still have power?"

"I do." I looked up at the round light in the kitchen ceiling to confirm this. "How about you?" I added, to be polite. Not waiting for her response, I took a breath. "Listen, I need you to do something for me."

I wasn't sure if Catherine was listening. "Our power's out," she informed me. "Since last night. We've called Nova Scotia Power. They said they'd be on it as soon as they can. But who am I to worry? I'm out here with an imposter survivalist, an electric generator, and a shed full of wood in a sea captain's house built before electricity. Working fireplaces in every room. And I have lots of eggs."

"Eggs?" I asked. I heard the racket of the generator in the background. Buildings that housed the public were advised to have an electrical backup that could last for at least seventy-two hours. Some places, like Seaview Manor, the seniors' residence, had several and could keep going even longer in any weather. Catherine would be fine, but I needed her attention.

"Yes. We had to bring the chickens in," Catherine rambled on. "We put them in the downstairs bathroom, but that didn't last. Simon let them out. They're making themselves at home now. Gareth's having a grand old time giving them names after Nordic goddesses. I've got Frejya following me around the kitchen, nagging for food. Skadi, the goddess of winter, is in the dining room. I sat down for a rest and broke an egg she laid behind a cushion. The cat's nerves are shot. So are mine."

"Sounds chaotic." I tried to sound sympathetic. "But I have an emergency. I need your help."

The word *help* worked. I could almost hear Catherine shift to high alert. Like all librarians, she was programmed to rise to any service occasion. It was part of her professional code.

"Sorry," she said. "That egg stain's going to be hard to get out of the brocade. What do you need?"

"It's a long story. I'll explain it all later, but Stuart and Harry are on their way to the look-off to check on the weather station. Stuart feels bad he underestimated this storm because he relied on misinformation. You know him, he can't stand anything he doesn't understand."

"I know the feeling," Catherine said. "But is that the emergency?"

"Sort of, but not really." Where was I going to start? "I am pretty sure that this storm-watcher guy staying at the motel killed Percy Skinner. And he could hurt Stuart and Harry if he runs into them at the look-off."

"Not sure I understand," Catherine said. "Listen, I've got eggs to find. Here's Rollie. I'll let him talk to you."

My cousin came on the line. "Everything okay?" he asked. "Do you still have power?"

"Yes, I have power. But Rollie, that's not why I called. Listen to me. I need someone to get over to the look-off. Stuart might be there with Harry. I need them to get back to town and not talk to anyone. I'll explain everything when they get here."

"Take it easy," Rollie said, pulling out his retired psychologist's soothing voice, the one that annoyed me. "What's this about?"

"No time, Rollie. Just get Stuart and Harry away from the look-off. It's important. Trust me." I thought of the knife they'd found in the bloody snowbank. I felt sick.

"Honestly, Valerie." Rollie sighed with resignation. "I tell you what: I've got Simon here. He's the one who liberated the chickens from the bathroom. Catherine would appreciate not seeing his face for a bit. He's outside walking around in some old snowshoes we found in the basement. I'll send him over to pass on your message to them. How about that?"

I considered this. Simon was a fanatic. That should motivate him enough to make it through the snow to the look-off.

"Thanks, Rollie," I said. "Tell him to hurry."

After I'd done all I could, I reverted to my own survival tactics. By the time my street was blown free of snow and the older men staggered home heroes, my freezer was short one plastic bag full of frozen brownies.

I was wiping the crumbs from my mouth when Harry's truck pulled up in front of the house. Toby heard it before

I did, leaped off the couch, and ran to the door. Stuart and Harry were on the steps. They came in through the door in a blast of cold air, stomped their feet on the mat, showered me with snow, and handed me jackets. Stuart's hands were red. Harry's face was wind chapped. They looked excited and pleased with themselves, like little boys coming in after an afternoon out making snow forts. If they'd met a murderer or had a brush with death, it didn't show.

"Jason Black," I said. "The storm chaser. Was he there?"

Stuart looked at me as if I had walked in from Mars, not up the hall in my own house. "No."

"Good," I could breathe again. "He's dangerous. I figured he'd go after you. I was scared."

Harry looked at Stuart. "You going to tell her, or should I?"

"Tell me what?" I asked.

"You figured it out, Dick Tracy," Harry said. "All on your own. Stuart filled Wade in on the way here. Don't think Wade has been this impressed since the Kings won the Stanley Cup in 2012 as the eighth-seeded team."

Stuart nodded in agreement and stepped in front of Harry, so he was close to me. I had no idea what they were talking about. None. He then walked past me and picked up the kettle, filled it at the sink, and opened the cupboard where I kept the box of tea. He knew his way around my kitchen.

Once the tea was made and poured, the three of us sat down at the kitchen table. "Okay, tell me everything," I said.

Stuart began to speak, but Harry took over.

"We should start with the snowplow," Harry said, "before you hear it from anyone else." He nodded toward the ancient tabletop radio on the kitchen counter. "Gasper's Cove has its snowplow back. I found it. Sort of a saved-the-day situation." He put down his mug. "Probably should get home and change. Media," he said to me, in case I didn't understand. "Interviews."

Stuart choked into a napkin. "The first question they're going to ask is what were you doing behind the fish plant."

Harry looked sideways in the direction of my front window, the street, and the snowblown piles. "I was there because of my regulars ...," he stopped.

"Regulars?" I remembered the mugs the snowblowing crew of retirees had put in the snow banks. It clicked. "A still? You have a *still* behind the fish plant? I don't believe it." But of course, I did. Moonshine had been a part of the coast even before the rum-running days. And Harry had a soft spot for the abandoned fish plant, the place one Christmas where he'd run a poinsettia grow-op. Harry specialized in never learning from his mistakes.

"You might call it a still," Harry admitted. "Anyways, I figured it would be a good idea to make a few deliveries before the storm set in. That's when I saw it."

"The snowplow?" I asked.

"Larger than life, behind the plant. Parked kind of crooked. Not how I would have done it. If I'd had the keys, I would have driven that sucker back down to town," Harry said. "Good with heavy equipment, from clearing the ice down at the rink. All I could do was call Wade and tell him where it was."

Stuart stepped in before Harry could continue. "Wade was up at the plant when he got my call—you know, the one you wanted me to make? About how you thought Jason Black was the snowplow thief?"

"He's that, but that's not all he is. Let me tell you ...," I began.

Stuart held up a hand. "Let me finish. This is the best part. After they got the plow back, Wade decided to drop by the Anchor to follow up on your idea. And guess what? You were right."

"I was?" I asked. About all of it? I wondered. "What happened?"

"This is the crazy part," Stuart said. "I guess when Wade showed up, Jason was in his motel room, editing video of himself in the plow. He claims he only borrowed it out of professional interest. He said as a severe weather watcher, he felt it was important that he could report firsthand on what it was like to handle emergency equipment. He planned to shoot some 'how-to drive a snowplow' video. He figured his followers would love it. But when he drove it up the hill, he realized the plow had more gears than he could handle. He lost his nerve. So, he ditched it, out of sight. He wanted to get the video up and leave town and then let us know where it was." Stuart reached over and took my hand. "If it wasn't for you, he might have gotten away with it. I think they're going to charge him with theft of municipal property and obstructing the delivery of essential services."

"Boy's next video's going to be shot in a room with bars on its windows," Harry said with satisfaction. "Bet on it."

"Wow," I said. "But the weather station? And Percy? Did they get anything out of Jason on that?"

"Weather is federal," Harry said with authority. "You don't mess with the feds. Never turns out too good."

"But Percy," I persisted. "It makes sense to me that he saw something. Maybe he caught Black messing around with the weather equipment. They were both at the Anchor the night Percy died. Black must be the one who killed him."

Stuart's grip on my hand tightened. "Valerie. Did you hear anything we said? You figured out who took the snowplow. Great achievement, everyone's grateful. But there is no evidence that Black had anything to do with the weather instrumentation. For a start, only a few people have the key. I got one because of the work I do with the municipality, but no way would a tourist have any access. The hut is kept locked. And this theory that Percy might have seen him up there, it doesn't mean anything,"

"But I saw Jason there myself," I protested, "the other day."

Stuart stopped me before I could continue. He put his hands on my shoulders.

"Valerie, it's called a look-off for a reason. People go there for the view, all times of day. That doesn't make them all killers, does it?"

"No, I guess not," I admitted.

"Well, there you go," Stuart said, patting my shoulder. "Look, Wade's got Black. If he's done anything more than steal a snowplow, the RCMP will figure it out. I think we're done for the day."

"True enough," Harry said, standing up. "Maybe I'll head out. Roads are getting better; I can get up the hill and pick up something to celebrate. I've got a couple of frozen pizzas in the back of the truck. They'd be good. Fire up the oven. What do you think?"

"Maybe another time," Stuart said. "You go ahead, Harry." He looked at me. "I'll find my own way home."

CHAPTER TWENTY-ONE

Stuart stayed late, and we talked.

"What did you think when Simon turned up?" I asked. We were settled on the couch, Toby up there beside us. "I was worried. Your cell wasn't connecting. I had this theory about Jason ... all I could think of was to call the Inn and have them find you. Sending Simon was Rollie's idea."

"Poor guy." Stuart shook his head. "He had his snowshoes on backward. It couldn't have been easy to make it to the look-off like that. But I knew who he was. I recognized his face from the back of the books?"

"Which books?"

"Erin's. She's a big fan of his series. I looked at a few to see what she read. Modern fantasy-type stories based on old folklore and myths. At least his novels got her out of the vampire craze. I never figured that one out."

Toby laid his head on Stuart's knee and snored. I didn't get the vampires either. "What kind of myths does he write about?"

"Celtic mostly, some Scandinavian, too, as far as I can tell. *The Revenge of the Valkyries* is her favorite."

"Valkyries?" I asked. Gareth had talked about them, but I couldn't remember what he said.

"Yes, those were the women who took care of the fallen warriors. Sort of a next-world intake team. They decided who had done a good job in battle and could go off and live with Odin. The rest went to some kind of hell. In Simon's version, Odin was an extraterrestrial," he laughed. "That didn't make a lot of sense to me, but I'm not a teenage girl."

This was true. Norse gods reminded me of the stone in Stuart's yard. I hadn't told him about Harry's scam or Danny's UNESCO scheme, so I did that now.

"Let me get this right: I have a grave headstone reject in the middle of my rock garden? Something that Harry Sutherland, who fixes up the ice at the rink, dumped with a load of fill? Well, that explains something."

"What?" I asked.

"Why Danny called. He said he heard about my big stone and wanted it back. I told him it was in deep, I had perennials around it, and unless he could give me a good reason why he needed it, it was staying in my rock garden." Stuart paused. "I guess that picture of Percy's that he shared at the meeting started this whole mess."

I felt a jolt of interest. This mattered. I knew it did. "When did Danny call you? Before Percy died, or after?"

"After," Stuart said. "That's what was strange. Who asks about a garden in the middle of winter?"

That was a very good question. I didn't have an answer, and neither did Stuart. We might have worked through that, and a few other things, but before we could, Stuart's phone, now in town range, rang.

Stuart looked at the number and then me. "Public Works. Got to take this."

I got up while he talked and took our empty tea mugs to the kitchen. Standing at the sink, I could hear Stuart's side of the conversation. It seemed that crews were working on the causeway, trying to get one lane open. The supervisor wanted Stuart's input as the consulting engineer.

Stuart joined me in the kitchen. "Sorry, Val. They need me down there. They're sending a truck for me. Let's take a rain check, or a snow check, or whatever you want to call it." He already had his parka on. "Let's finish this another time," he said, reaching out. The tightly woven fabric of his weatherproof jacket circled my shoulders.

'Take care," I said. "It's icy out there." No one could blame me for wishing we had been snowed in.

"Don't worry," Stuart said, reaching down to ruffle Toby's head. "I know what I'm doing."

Well, I thought, at least one of us does.

After Stuart left, the house felt even emptier than it had when I was alone. I'd spent most of my life living with someone and had made a huge effort since coming back to Gasper's Cove to learn how to live alone. And now, just when I thought I was good at it, I wondered if it suited me. I had a long night ahead. I wanted company, a voice to talk to in my silent, empty house. I picked up my phone and considered calling Darlene but decided her honeymoon had had more than its share of interruptions.

I decided the next best thing for me to do was knit.

I settled into my chair and started my second sock. It was repetitive knitting, not thinking knitting, soothing and stabilizing, exactly what I needed. Outside, I could hear the recovered plow down the hill, no doubt working its way along Front Street to the partially opened causeway. I turned on the radio. CKGC told me that the worst was behind us and that the schools would reopen the day after tomorrow.

I dropped my knitting needle on the floor.

I didn't pick it up but reached for my phone instead. Why hadn't I thought of this before?

After two rings, Noah answered.

"Hey, Val, what's up?" he asked.

"What's up is I am talking to you," I answered, as I always did. "Do you have a minute? Time for a quick question?"

"I have many minutes. I want to talk to you too. You first."

"You do some work now and then for CKGC, don't you?" I asked.

"Sure, time to time, cover for the regular guys when they need me. Why?"

"The local weather reports. Tell me how those work. Some volunteer goes out to the weather station and checks it? Calls you?"

"They used to do that, but now the results are uploaded to the cloud, and a program puts it into an AI script."

"AI?" I asked.

"Artificial intelligence. Basically, the software translates the numbers into words."

I tried to translate this process into something that made sense to me. "Tell me if I am right about this: The program automatically comes up with the weather report from the numbers the instruments save to the Internet?"

"You got it."

I could see the problems with this system. The holes in it were large enough for anyone with common sense, rarer these days than degrees in computer science, to see.

"The Internet in Gasper's Cove comes and goes," I pointed out. "Particularly in the winter. Not only during storms. The Northern Lights can knock it out too. I heard that down at the lineup at the Foodmart."

"That's a theory about the Lights," Noah admitted. "And there is some science behind that."

"So, how would the station get information from the weather station if the Internet was out? When the weather was really bad?" I asked. I was adjusting to the idea that this interference didn't come down to a key and a hut.

"Good question," Noah said. "I don't do a lot at CKGC, but I was there when the new system went online. It's standard software; I've got a buddy in Halifax who works with it. I'll text him and see what he says. I'll get back to you."

"Thank you." I was skeptical. In my experience, removing the human element did not guarantee progress. "I'll let you go now," I said.

"Whoa, Valerie, wait." There was a different tone in Noah's voice—what he wanted to tell me was personal, not work-related. "Have you listened to the podcast?" he asked.

"I don't listen to those much," I said. "A couple on sewing and knitting. Stuart had me try one on dog-training." I hadn't told Stuart, but I hadn't made it through the first episode. Toby already knew how to come, sit, and stay. That was all I needed, and all he could think about. "But I guess with someone we know in the business, I should listen to more."

"Yeah, well. I'll send you a link." Noah paused and then added, "I wonder how Kay feels about this."

My phone dinged in my hand. That was fast. "Got it," I said. "I'll listen to it right now."

"Do that," Noah said. "I've been trying to reach him to verify what he said, but he's not answering my calls. Tell me what you think."

"Of course," I said, moving to the laptop on the dining-room table, closing the link to an online fabric sale, opening my messages, and tapping the link so I could keep talking. Tristan's face appeared on my screen, his beautiful hair falling over one eye, catching the photographer's light. Beneath it, I read:

EPISODE 423: Is the killer of Magnus Einarsson hiding in Gasper's Cove, Nova Scotia?

"Noah," I said, "I'll call you back."

CHAPTER TWENTY-TWO

I turned up the volume on my laptop and listened. At the same time, I used my phone to do a quick search for Magnus Einarsson. I had never heard the name before, but I sure had heard of Gasper's Cove.

The information on Einarsson was limited, with no references in the last three decades. Before that, there had been a few papers published by the young Icelandic academic, mostly on the theory that the Viking settlement in L'Anse, Newfoundland, had led to further exploration down the coast of Nova Scotia, and even into Maine. His work had been referred to a few times, mainly by bloggers and treasure hunters, but as far as I could make out, no one had heard from him in years.

In the background, the ad and introduction ended. Tristan repeated the title of his episode and continued:

> *Thirty years ago, a promising young archeologist named Magnus Einarsson came to an obscure community in the small and remote province of Nova Scotia, following the trail of Viking explorers. His search led him to a*

desolate location, following rumors that evidence of Norse habitation, including rune stones, could be found there.

Unfortunately, Einarsson arrived at a disruptive time. His archeological work was interrupted by the construction of a land connection, a causeway, between this backward community and the mainland, resulting in excavation near his dig. The conflict between the two projects may have escalated if Einarsson hadn't suddenly disappeared. No one thought anything of it—after all, the community had many newcomers employed on the building project, and they came and went.

But, the questions remain.

No one heard from Magnus Einarsson again. Not the academic journals he submitted to, not the conferences he was supposed to attend. He was a man who traveled a lot, had studied in both Norway and the US, but seemed to have few personal connections.

Maybe no one found him because no one looked.

Until now. Over the coming episodes, I will be continuing my own exploration to find answers to these questions:

- *What was Magnus Einarsson searching for?*
- *Did he find it?*
- *Did that discovery have anything to do with his disappearance?*
- *He had enemies in this community. If he had made a significant archeological find, would work on the causeway have been stopped?*
- *Why did a committed researcher with a bright future vanish without a trace? Did he give up his career of his own free will?*

• Or was he murdered? And is the murderer still there?

Magnus Einarsson deserves his peace. And Solved and Resolved is committed to speaking his truth. No one can heal and move on if they never know what happened.

My phone slipped out of my shaking hands. I picked it up and dialed my daughter.

"Mom?"

I decided to start this conversation with the truth. "I listened to the podcast," I said. "Did you know about this?"

"I do now." She stopped talking and blew her nose. "I met Tristan at a Canadian Thanksgiving party a friend in Aberdeen gave in the fall. He wanted to hear all about where I grew up. It never occurred to me that it was Gasper's Cove, not me, he was interested in." Kay took a big breath. I detected more anger than hurt in her voice. This was a good thing. She was her mother's daughter.

"What did he have to say for himself?" I asked.

"Not much," Kay admitted. "We had a big fight. I did most of the talking." Definitely my daughter. "He said he cared about me, but that his job was to make sure justice was served." She laughed, but without humor. "Particularly in time to score a new advertiser."

"What happens now?" I asked, with a silent apology to Darlene. If anyone had hurt my daughter, it absolutely was my business. "What are you going to do?"

"Not sure. Tristan's not here. He texted someone and said he had a meeting. No idea who, or what it's about. All I know is that it is more important to him than our relationship."

"Kay, I'm so sorry. Do you want me to come over?" I asked.

"No, Mom, I'm okay. Darlene and George will be home soon. I want to clean the place up. I think I need some time by myself to process. Do you understand?"

"I do," I said, and I did. Sort of. "You need anything, call. Promise? I love you."

"Love you too."

My next call was to Noah. His line was busy, so I left a message. I told him that I had listened to the podcast, that Kay hadn't known about any of this, and that if Tristan knew what was good for him, he had better hope he didn't run into me. Deceiving one Rankin woman was trouble enough; two, and he'd better look out. Generations raising families on this rocky coast in this kind of weather did not produce women who put up with nonsense.

Or mothers who sat still and waited.

I went into the kitchen and made a pot of tea. I let it steep until it was dark and black before I poured it. That gave me time to think.

This story of Magnus Einarsson was new information. I opened my junk drawer, found an envelope to write on, and, after five tries, found a pen that had ink. I made a list:

1. Thirty years ago, when the causeway was being built, an archeologist called Magnus Einarsson came to town.
2. He is interested in rocks. Runes are rocks that are proof the Vikings were here.
3. The boys working on the causeway were hauling rocks. One of them was Percy Skinner, who did something with his truck and seriously hurt some locals.

4. This Magnus goes missing. Never heard from again. Was he killed? By who? Why?
5. Thirty years later, Percy disappears, presumed dead too. What happened to him? Is there a connection?
6. A jerky podcaster is meeting someone. Who? Why?

I added milk to my bitter tea and studied my list. Two whos? Two whys? Trying to organize my thoughts wasn't working. I tried intuition next. I looked down at Toby and thought about dogs, the one on my kitchen floor and the smaller one over in Drummond at Stuart's house. I had been so occupied with the distractions, the missing snowplow, the weather reports, the ornamental tombstone in a garden, I had overlooked the most important element of the Duck Toller's dance: the way that breed of hunting dog didn't go after the birds but distracted them with movement. And the reason for it was the hunter in the bushes. The watcher.

That's who mattered.

I went back to the beginning. This all started when Percy vanished. But there was nothing in Percy's current life, searching beaches for coins, attending monthly meetings of amateur treasure hunters, that would make him worth killing. Therefore, the reason he was gone—the knife—had to lie in the past. But what did I know about Percy's past, except he had worked on the causeway, hauling rocks about the time Magnus Einarsson had gone missing?

I tried to see that time in my mind. Percy had dumped a load of rocks too early. Was that an accident or intentional? If he'd meant to do it, why? I had a flash. Maybe he wanted to bury something or someone. A citizen or the scholar who opposed the causeway project? Was Percy himself a killer or a witness to someone who was? I focused hard to see that day, but all I could make out were shadows. Only someone who was there at the time would know what really had happened. But who would that be?

I knew.

I picked up my phone again and called my cousin Rollie.

CHAPTER TWENTY-THREE

"Do you have power?" my cousin asked instead of saying hello. "Do you need eggs?"

"Yes, I have power. No, I don't need eggs," I answered. "But I have a question. About Gareth."

"Gareth?" Rollie asked. "You just missed him. Do you want to leave a message?"

"No, that's all right. I don't need to talk *to* Gareth, I want to talk *about* him. Tell me again how you met."

"I was his student when I first went to university. Archeology was an elective. Gareth was a great teacher. He treated me like an equal. He knew where I was from, how I was a rural boy in the big town. We kept in touch, even when I changed disciplines." I could hear the smile in my cousin's voice. Whatever he was now, in his heart, he, too, would always be an academic.

He was also in the mood to give me the details I needed. "You mentioned, I think, that he'd been to Gasper's Cove on a project himself," I prompted him. "Do you have any idea when?"

"Decades ago. He came to do some excavation work on a dig, but they didn't find anything. Gareth wasn't here long," Rollie said. "He remembers crossing on one of the last ferries."

The causeway. It was a link not only between two communities but, it seemed now, between the secrets of the past and the present. "Probably the last summer before the causeway opened," I suggested, "about the time Magnus Einarsson disappeared?"

"Magnus who?" Rollie asked. "The name's familiar, but I can't quite place it."

"Exactly. That is the point, right there. He was an archeologist who disappeared a long time ago." The idea percolating in my mind bubbled over. "Do you think Gareth knew him?"

"Possibly," Rollie admitted. "You'd have to ask him. All I knew was, the project Gareth worked on was a bust. A bit of an embarrassment for the team, if I remember correctly. That's why Gareth was let go. And maybe why this Magnus faded away. Things didn't work out."

"You said Gareth isn't there," I said. "Off for a walk? In this snow?"

"No, in the car," Rollie said. "He got picked up. Some kind of consultation."

"Do you know where he went?" I asked. Tristan had gone to meet someone—maybe a person connected with a cold case as old as the causeway. "Was he with Tristan?"

"You mean that friend of Kay's?" Rollie sounded puzzled. "No, it wasn't him. I got to say, it was nice for him to go out for lunch. Although over at the Anchor, not so sure if the food will be up to Gareth's standards."

"The Anchor?" I asked. "Why there?"

"Your guess is as good as mine," Rollie said. "Fish-and-chips. Not sure they've ever changed the oil in that fryer. But what can you say? That's Danny."

"Danny?"

"Yes, didn't I tell you?" Rollie asked. "That's who came to pick Gareth up. He had something to show him."

After I let Rollie go, I went outside to the truck. My mind was full of colliding ideas. I didn't understand this lunch. Why would a wannabe tourism entrepreneur want to meet with a real expert today? And what would he say to Gareth that he couldn't have asked the last time they had met, the night Percy went missing?

This made no sense. None at all.

And where, come to think of it, was Tristan? That was a good question.

One of many I had.

It was slow going across the causeway. The roads were partially clear now but backed up at the entry to the single lane across the water. I felt for the poor road worker, dressed in so many layers that he looked like a snowman in a reflective vest, trying to direct traffic, a walkie-talkie in one hand and a sign he rotated between *Stop* and *Slow* in the other. Waiting my turn gave me time to think. The way to the Anchor would take me past the RCMP detachment. I wondered if I should drop in and see Wade. But what would I say to him? That a retired professor and a motel manager were having fish-and-chips? No, that wasn't enough.

My brain felt stuck. The car behind me honked. The *Stop* sign had turned to *Slow*. I stepped on the gas, lurched forward, bumped down the ramp, and crossed into Drummond. Ahead of me, I saw the flags of the RCMP detachment.

I kept driving.

If I found out something at the Anchor that was important, then I would go and see Wade. It wasn't much of a plan. But it was the only plan I had.

I never made it into the motel. When I pulled into the parking lot, I skidded on the ice and almost ran over Gareth, who was standing near a snowbank.

"Oh, you," he said, when I rolled down the window to apologize for almost hitting him. "I called a taxi, but you're here first. Quick," he said, pulling on the passenger door of the truck. "Get me out of here. The man is insane."

I jumped out, helped him in, and drove back out onto the main road. Beside me, Gareth was pale and shaking.

"What's going on?" I asked, wondering if helping the professor escape had been the right thing to do.

Gareth didn't answer. Instead, he wiped the frost from his window and peered behind us through the side-view mirror. "Move," he said. "He might follow us. Take me right into town."

I swiped a sideways look at Gareth. He looked older, frailer, almost desperate.

"Are you okay?" I asked. We were close to Drummond Consolidated. "We're almost at the hospital. Maybe we should stop?"

"No, keep going." Gareth laid a hand on my shoulder. His grip was stronger than I expected. "I don't want to go near that causeway quite yet. The Inn's the first place he'd go."

My phone beeped on the console between us and lit up. I had a message. From Stuart. I wanted to stop and read it. Ahead in the growing dark, I saw the road that led into Drummond's small industrial park had been cleared. I flicked on my indicator and drove up to the blank face of Acme Fasteners.

I shifted into park, took off my gloves, and picked up my phone, but then turned to Gareth.

"I think you need to tell me what's going on," I said.

Gareth loosened the scarf around his neck. "That man is a fool. He wanted me to authenticate some of the rubbish in his display as genuine. He wanted to pay me." Gareth snorted. "That pile of junk. I was insulted. My reputation is everything to me. Everything. I told him I wanted to leave. He wouldn't take no for an answer. He got quite insistent. Fortunately, there was some issue at the front desk. When he went to deal with it, I called a ride and went out the side door to wait. Then, you came."

Gareth's face tried to smile, but even in the dim glow from the tall light beside the building, his eyes looked haunted.

I didn't know how to respond. Snowflakes against the windshield and a gust of wind rocked the car. Somewhere on the road behind us, I heard a siren. An ambulance on the way to the hospital? The RCMP?

I put my phone in my lap and turned the car heater up to high. I reached for my gloves, then remembered the message from Stuart. I picked the phone up and with my right thumb opened the message.

> Tristan is here. He says an archeologist was murdered here years ago. He thinks the body is somewhere under the causeway. He wanted to talk to me about excavation. BTW, he is sure Gareth was involved. What do you think?

I was aware of the retired professor beside me, watching.

I felt weak, as all the energy in my body had pulled back and gathered in my chest. How I handled this mattered.

"My daughter," I said, as casually as a woman in a car in a deserted industrial park with a possible murderer could say it. I let the phone fall into my lap, and I reached for the gear shift with my right hand. I wiped the inside of the windshield and looked up at the building. "Acme Fasteners," I said. "Not very original."

Out on the highway, I heard the sirens again. My hopes lifted and then, as they faded away, fell.

I could feel Gareth studying me. "That wasn't your daughter, was it? Who was that message from? What did it say?"

I was no liar and worse under pressure.

"It was from Stuart. Kay's podcaster friend figured it out. I know you were here years ago." Gareth's hands were tight on his cane. I had caught the old archeologist off guard. I couldn't stop now. "They know. You're caught, or at least about to be. Tristan figures you killed that Magnus and hid his body somehow during the construction of the causeway. Your secret's out." I felt some kind of victory in delivering this news, but then I thought of the siren and Gareth's quick getaway from the motel. Had something happened to Danny? Had Gareth killed him too? Was I, alone in the dark under the lights of Acme Fasteners, going to be next?

My mind didn't know where to stop, and neither did my mouth. "I bet you found something—was that it? And you wanted the credit for the discovery to be yours." Finally, it was coming together, even though that meant I now had every reason to be very afraid of this man in my truck.

But instead of arguing, or attacking me, Gareth slumped in his seat.

"Oh my. How could you think that? Of me?" he asked. "I didn't kill anyone. Not years ago, not here, not on any site. And not Magnus. And I can tell you that."

I was cold. Terror made me even colder. I started to shake.

"Tell that to the RCMP," I said, with more courage than I felt.

"I will," Gareth said. "I have absolute proof I didn't kill Magnus Einarsson."

"You do?"

"Yes. You see my dear, that's who I am."

CHAPTER TWENTY-FOUR

"What?" I stared at the man next to me in the truck.

"Yes, I'm Magnus Einarsson," Gareth said, almost wistfully. "You know, it's lovely to say my name out loud to someone after all of these years."

"I don't understand," I said. I didn't. I had an overwhelming desire for something chocolate. I could almost taste it.

"This day had to happen. I always knew that," Gareth said. "Maybe that's what brought me here. Rollie knows everything. I saw him a few times years ago, professionally, when he was in private practice as a psychologist. Confidentiality and all of that. I knew him. I trusted him. I had to share my secret with someone. When the pressure to close the circle at this stage of my life began to build, I knew I would need his help again, to get through it."

This explained so much. The close attention Rollie had given Gareth. Catherine had nothing to worry about. Rollie wasn't bored with life at the Inn; he was only trying to help someone else.

"All right, this sounds like Rollie," I conceded. "What I don't understand is how this all started. Why did you pretend to be someone else?"

"Pride goeth before the fall," Gareth answered. "And I believe the present moment would be the fall. I was so ambitious at that stage of my career. I was convinced that Viking explorers had come this far south. I funded my own project, such as it was, and hired a few students to work for me. And then, when I saw the big rocks they laid down as a base for the causeway, I had this idea that at least some of them were artifacts, runes. I don't think this was wishful thinking, either. To this day, I am sure I saw something of great value, but before I could verify that fact, the material had been hauled away as fill. I was beside myself, as you can imagine. I tried to stop one of the trucks and force it off the road. There was an accident. I was too late, anyway." He paused to stare out the window into the black. "It was the rune's destiny not to reveal itself. I had to accept my part in that story. History, like the Valkyries themselves, had touched down, made its decision, and moved on. So, I decided to leave Magnus Einarsson, a failed archeologist, with them. I needed a new identity, of course, so I added an invented name—Gareth Davies sounded distinguished—to the list of research assistants on the last paper I submitted as Einarsson. Then, I made myself disappear and then reappear as Gareth." He looked over at me. "I'd given him a boost, of course. Credit in a peer-reviewed journal, even as a research assistant, is a credible start to any academic career."

I tried to process this. "You made up a name, put it in a paper for publication, and *became* that person?" I tried and failed to imagine how it would feel to become someone else. I had lived my own life surrounded by people who knew me and knew my family, immediate, extended, and related. Anonymity in Nova Scotia was not possible. No matter where you went, someone's aunt's cousin's sister's best friend would recognize you for sure. I wondered if not having those connections left a vacancy in a soul that would make a new identity plausible.

"That sounds like a lot of work," I said. "And a lot of risk to undo it. Why?" I was still unclear about Percy, and that bothered me a lot. What was his place, or fate, in this story?

"I was haunted," Gareth admitted. "The irony of my career eventually overcame me. I was spending so much of my time on the truth, verifying artifacts, uncovering frauds and fakes, but that's what I was myself. I think what brought me back here was that this was the last place where I was me. There was also that feeling ... I always wondered, maybe it was real, maybe it is still here."

"Do you mean the rune?" I asked. "Not just your own identity, but the rune? Did you ever find any evidence of it again?"

"No. All I saw was a photo. An amateur attempt, certainly, but there was an obsession behind it"—he paused—"an obsession that made me realize I wasn't the only one who couldn't let go."

"Percy," I breathed. "Percy Skinner. He was the driver on the causeway who had the accident. Am I right? Did he recognize you? Is that why you killed him?" A ritual killing, Gareth had said at the time, using an old knife, like the one a Treasure Trover might have brought to a meeting. A weapon that would take more skill than force to use.

"Killed? The man they say was murdered? Don't be foolish. I am a scholar, not a killer. Besides, I don't think he recognized me. I'm old. Even if he had recognized me, there would be some relief in that. At a certain age, who you *were* doesn't matter anyway. Life forgets you before it lets you go. I never touched the man."

I wasn't sure if I should believe him, but I couldn't sit there all night trying to figure that out. Gareth seemed authentic. Rollie trusted him. I guessed that counted for something. I held my breath, shifted into reverse, and backed out of the lot and onto the main road. I waited for Gareth to act, but instead, he sighed and closed his eyes. I tightened my hands on the wheel and kept my eyes on the road and the lights of the town ahead. I needed to hear more. I needed to know how unsafe I was. Gareth liked to talk. I would keep him talking.

"You were the last person to see Percy alive," I said. "You told me that yourself."

Beside me, Gareth blinked and resurfaced into the present.

"I thought I was. During our little smoke break, I had a good look at Percy. That's when I realized who he was." The professor turned to me, his self-confidence gone, replaced by a plea for understanding. "I made up my mind right there and then to share my real identity. I decided if he figured it out, telling my own story was the only way to preserve my dignity. But he had to go meet someone. I didn't get the chance."

My head snapped around to look at Gareth. Meet someone?

"Who?" I asked. I thought of the blood on the snow. "Didn't you tell the RCMP this?"

"No, because they didn't ask." Gareth sounded annoyed. "When you're older, no one thinks you know anything useful. It's worse for women. Just you wait." I could feel him studying me. "The Old Norse were wiser than we are," he said. "They understood the sources of power. This month, I have felt Skadi's presence."

"Skadi?" I asked. Did Gareth have premonitions like I did?

"The goddess," Gareth explained, "of winter and hunting."

I turned up the car heater. I felt a chill. "Did Percy say who he was meeting?" I asked to change the subject.

"I can't recall," Gareth admitted. "An interview? A young man? The radio?"

"Noah?" Why hadn't the young reporter told me about this?

"No, I've met Noah. And I would have remembered a biblical name," Gareth assured me. "It was someone else, a person who worked with whales, I think."

"Whales?" I asked. "Are you sure?" I wondered what stress had done to Gareth's worn brain.

"Yes, I am." Gareth was definite. "Like dolphins. They are the only species who ..."

I finished his sentence for him: "... travel in pods." I felt sick to my stomach. "Is there any chance Percy told you he was meeting a *podcaster*?" I said the word slowly, hoping I was wrong.

"My dear, you've got it!" Gareth beamed at me as if I were a student who had given him the right answer. "That's exactly what he said. But I still don't understand why Percy went off to meet an environmentalist."

With one hand on the wheel, I pulled my phone from my pocket and threw it to Gareth. I explained to him how to go into my messages and asked him to read out loud the last one from Stuart.

Tristan is here. He says an archeologist was murdered here years ago. He thinks the body is somewhere under the causeway. He wanted to talk to me about excavation. BTW, he is sure Gareth was involved. What do you think?

Gareth held the phone out at arm's length, as if to see if the message would read differently from a distance. "I am most offended. Who is this Tristan person to slander me?"

"The podcaster Percy was supposed to meet. A podcast is like a radio show," I added. My chest felt tight. My next words stuck in my throat. "If you didn't kill Percy, Tristan did," I said, trying out the idea. As soon as I heard it, I knew I was right. "But why?"

Gareth drew into himself and sat for a moment. "Loki," he finally pronounced.

"Loki?" I asked. The name had a vague comic-book familiarity to it. "Who is he?"

"The Norse god of deceit. A shapeshifter and troublemaker." Gareth's voice took on a practiced lecturer tone. "Never to be trusted."

And trusting him was exactly what my daughter had done. My intuition had been right. In ten minutes, depending on the roads, we would be where I needed to go. My headlights caught the speed-limit sign. I ignored it.

"Tristan is like Loki?" I asked, leaning forward to get a better view of the road.

"Exactly. You have a rigorous mind," Gareth observed. "Have you ever considered a career in academia?" He glanced back at my phone. "Do you want me to read the next message from this Stuart?" he asked.

"Next message?" I asked, raising my voice above the sound of the heater.

"Yes." Gareth slid his glasses down his nose to get a better look at the small screen. "'*Just tolling. Can't wait for our date, still at the office. I'll have a hot and sour soup and order me a number 4.*' Strange message," Gareth said. "What's a number four?"

Tolling. What Duck Tollers like little Birdie were trained to do. Distract and stall so the hunter could move in on the prey. Stuart was in trouble. And it was Monday. Our favorite restaurant in Drummond was closed.

"You didn't play hockey?" I asked.

"No, chess," Gareth answered. "What does that have to do with anything? Do *you* play ice hockey?"

"No, but what country is this? I had kids." I veered left just before the lights changed at the first intersection back into town. It was beginning to snow again. "Number four belonged to Bobby Orr. The National Hockey League's most famous Canadian defenseman." I took the turn so fast that my fender bumped off a mountain of cleared snow. "Call the RCMP. The number is in my contacts," I ordered my passenger. "Stuart wants us to get Wade."

CHAPTER TWENTY-FIVE

"Are we no longer talking mythology?" Gareth asked from the seat beside me.

"That depends on who you ask," I said. "In 1970, Bobby Orr won the first Stanley Cup in 29 years for the Boston Bruins. With one goal. He flew through the air. There's a statue of it outside the Boston Gardens arena. Orr was a defenseman who played offense," I explained. "Same as Wade was for our local team. Did you find the number of the RCMP detachment?"

"I think I understand," Gareth said, lifting the phone. "Every culture has its mythology. Who do I ask for?"

"Officer Corkum," I said. "Wade Corkum was the greatest hockey player Gasper's Cove ever produced. That's what Stuart was trying to tell me. He needs the RCMP. Now. Fast."

Gareth nodded and repeated the address of Stuart's office to the officer on the phone. My calls to the detachment were never taken this seriously, but that didn't worry me now. Gareth was getting results. That was all that mattered.

The next call I asked Gareth to make was to Stuart, who didn't pick up. That worried me. A lot. As I drove through the snowy streets toward Stuart's office, I hoped Wade would arrive before me.

I turned onto Adelaide Street. Ahead, I saw the neon sign of the Peking Restaurant and, above it, the faint light of the offices on the second floor. I couldn't see if an RCMP cruiser was in front of the building; my view was obstructed by a giant, snorting, snow-vomiting, lights-flashing, beeping, Town of Drummond, never-stolen snowplow. It was moving so slowly down the street, it might as well have been moving backward, blocking me from reaching the decent man who had asked for my help and whom I didn't, under any circumstances, want to let down.

Gareth smoothed his fine woolen scarf around his neck and arranged the folds of his coat. "Looks like we're going to be here for a bit," he offered.

"I don't think so," I said. "Not me." I snapped off my seat belt, zipped my parka up to the top, and pulled my two-layer, double-knit, Shetland aran-weight hat down to below my eyebrows. "You'll be okay?" I asked my passenger. "I'll leave the car running, heater on. Be back as soon as I can." My hand was on the car-door handle, but I hesitated. Gareth looked tired and vulnerable. "I have to go," I said.

He read my mind. "Of course you do. Don't forget who I am: Magnus Einarsson. I was born in Iceland. I think I can cope with this."

"All right," I said. "You keep my phone and call the detachment back. See what is keeping Officer Corkum." I climbed out of the truck and caught the door before the wind could blow it open even wider.

I assessed my route. The Peking and Stuart's office were only half a block away. I couldn't get past the snowplow by walking on the street—that would be tight as well as dangerous. Plus, snow was now falling fast, visibility vanishing by the minute. Snowbanks on either side of the recently cleared road were chest-high and unbroken. But beyond them, the drifts on the sidewalks wouldn't be as deep, protected as they were by the two and three stories of the sea captains' residences that had been turned into professional offices. If I could get over the banks and stayed near the shelter of the buildings, I could make my way to Stuart's office. I pulled my hat down lower and tucked my pants into the top of my winter boots. I eyed the mountain range of snow in front of me. Thirty-five years ago, Darlene and I would have dug tunnels through snow like this for fun. But this was an emergency. Stuart's message had been a code for help.

I attacked the bank. Using a technique that had been effective the last time I had used it—in Grade 5—I slammed my boots into the hard wall of snow to make footholds and then tried to climb over the top. I slid down back to street level a few times and tried again. Finally, I made it up and over, skidding down the other side in my insulated nylon jacket like a human sled.

After landing, I got to my feet and looked down the street. Ahead, the neon sign of the Peking Restaurant called to me like a compass. I staggered toward it, narrowing my eyes against the flakes of snow.

The snow on what had been a sidewalk was soft under my boots. It made me think of stories of lost winter travelers, those who had let themselves lie down for a rest and then were found later, smiling, but frozen solid. I felt sympathy for them. I was exhausted. But I kept going, focused on the sign above the Chinese restaurant, until it, like the streetlights, flashed and went dead.

The power was out.

Oblivious, the snowplow continued relentlessly, lit by its own lights, leaving me alone on the street, in the dark.

I didn't stop. I didn't have a choice. I waded on through the snow, thigh-high next to the buildings, waist-high around the bushes, my hands feeling for walls and fences when I could find them, for support.

But I made it. When I reached the building, I pushed the glass door that led to the staircase up to the offices and, when that didn't work, pulled. There was movement, but not much. I looked down at the snow blown and drifted against the double glass. There, I saw footprints, one set going in, the indentations nearly gone, and others, more recent, coming out. Someone had gone into this building and had left.

I was scared. Was the door locked? What if Stuart needed me, and I couldn't get to him? I bent down and, with both mittened hands, started digging frantically, like Toby in the backyard, throwing the snow behind me, working with the light of the moon on the white snow, cursing the men in the plow, now down some side street. Tears froze on my cheeks, but I kept digging in the dark. I tried the door again. This time, it opened, but only halfway. I angled my body sideways, sucked in my breath, let the door compress my jacket-padded breasts, and wiggled myself into the building.

On the other side, I stopped and listened.

Nothing.

The restaurant beside me was dark. So were the stairs to the second floor. I knocked my boots together to shake off the worst of the snow and then, as quietly as a frozen woman could move, I started up the stairs, guided by the glow of an emergency light in the ceiling, my mitts on the railing, no idea what I was going to do when I got to the top.

Once there, I looked down the hall to Stuart's office. The door was open and swaying. From it, I felt cold, outside air, rolling toward me like a wave, or a warning.

This didn't look good. It felt even worse.

"Stuart!" I called as I ran down the hall. "Stuart! Are you okay?"

There was no answer.

I went through the door and into the office, through the reception area, past the three battered chairs and the collection of old sailing magazines, knocking into the second-hand coffee table as I passed, and into the next room.

I stopped. Even with only the faint light from the hall behind me, I could see the place was a mess. Half-unrolled sheaves of large engineering drawings covered the desk as if they had been thrown there, with more blown onto the floor. The wind pushed into me. I could see why: The window in this second-story office was open.

My snowy boots skidded on the papers on the floor as I made my way over to the window to shut it. It was a new unit, double-glazed, Stuart had once explained, to meet the Canadian Standards Association energy rating for thermal efficiency.

Not that the window was efficient now. It was wide open, letting in the snow.

I took off my mitt and reached out to pull the handle on the window frame in. As I did that, I looked out, and my mitt fell two stories down.

To land next to the still, spread-eagle, dark figure of a man in the snow.

CHAPTER TWENTY-SIX

I'll never remember what I did next, but somehow I found my way into the narrow side yard next to the building, only slightly aware of the sound of a siren behind me. Was it an ambulance? The RCMP? I should have cared, but I didn't. All I saw was the figure flat on the snow.

I called his name again as I made my way through the drifts to Stuart. The snow grabbed onto my legs and tried to hold me back. A cloud went over the moon and moved away.

"Val? You got my message." The dark crumple of clothing stirred on the ground. "I knew you'd figure it out. But where's Wade?"

"No idea," I said, then remembered the siren. "On his way, I hope." I made my way over to where Stuart lay and stood over him. "More to the point, what are you doing here?" I looked up at the window. I had forgotten to close it.

In response, Stuart spread his arms and legs out wider and started to move them slowly, in and out, up and down. "What does it look like? I'm making snow angels." Stuart Campbell, consulting engineer, giggled.

It was too much for me.

The stress of my ride and conversation with Gareth, the message on my phone, finding Stuart's office empty, and seeing him down here had put me over capacity a long time ago. I was done, so I did what I felt like: I turned my back to Stuart, let myself go, and fell back into the embrace of the snow. I spread my arms and legs wide and moved them up and down, in and out.

"Two can play at that game," I said. Snow angels had always been a specialty of mine. When this one was outlined perfectly, I asked Stuart, "What's with the open window? You fall out?" I thought this would be a very un-Stuart-like thing to happen.

"Fall?" Stuart giggled again, from the shock, or maybe the humor. "More like I was pushed," he said. "I sure hope Kay isn't serious about that guy. She could do better."

We agreed on that.

"Make it simple," I said. "What happened?" I reached over and took Stuart's hand in my remaining mitt. He had his jacket on, but it was unzipped; he probably hadn't had the time to do it up or put on his hat or gloves before he exited his office through the window. He must be cold.

"Do up your coat," I said. Once a Canadian mother, always a Canadian mother.

Stuart did as he was told. The giggling stopped. "Tristan called me and wanted to come to the office. He wanted to see the original drawings of the causeway construction. You know, the ones I have framed in my office?"

I knew exactly what he was talking about. Stuart's walls, at work and at home, were decorated with technical drawings of his interests: historical patents, sailing specs, and construction diagrams.

"I do," I said, moving my free arm and legs to keep warm. The snow kept falling. If we stayed here much longer, they wouldn't find us until spring. "Why was he interested in those?"

"I could see right away he had an agenda," Stuart began. "He wanted to know what Percy's job had been on the project. That was the first red flag. Then, he started recording when we were talking. That didn't feel right to me. He started to coach me. He'd ask a question, like 'Would you say?,' and then put words into my mouth."

"Like what? Give me an example."

"Okay. The one that got my attention was when he wanted me to say that it would have been possible to have hidden anything under the rocks they put down for the base. He laughed as if it was a joke and asked, 'Even a body?' He wanted to take my drawings." I felt Stuart's hand go tight in mine. "He asked me how much it would cost to mark up the specs with an X where the rock slide had been, something an engineer would know, and where a body could have been covered up. He wanted to imply that someone on site at the time had been suspicious. I told him I didn't believe what he was asking me to do. And he said everyone has a price. That's when I knew he was real trouble. And I texted you."

"Pretty risky," I said, "your message. Why didn't you call Wade yourself if you were worried?"

"I couldn't," Stuart said. "Tristan was right with me, watching over my shoulder. I told him you would be coming to meet me, and I needed to put you off for a bit." He squeezed my hand again. "I know how your mind works. I knew you'd get it. And I thought if something happened to me, I wanted him caught."

I couldn't say anything to that. I just couldn't. "But the window?"

"He grabbed the drawings, then pulled out a knife. He backed me up to the window, made me open it." Stuart laughed. "You know what was the only thing I could think of? Why had I been in such a hurry to bring those old windows up to code? It would have been safer when it was painted shut."

The flurries had eased up. It was so quiet. I wondered why it was like that in the winter, if the snow absorbed the sound. "But I don't understand," I said. "Why did he push you?"

"It's obvious," Stuart said. "He was trying to kill me. He'd tried to bribe me, and I'd turned him down. If that had gotten out, what was left of his reputation would be gone." Stuart paused and moved closer to me. "My big mouth didn't help. I asked him what happened to Percy. And as soon as I said that, we both knew I'd figured it out—that Percy vanishing like that was awfully convenient for a guy trying to build up a story. But Tristan isn't as smart as he thinks he is. My sense is that he's losing it, trying to cover his tracks, but things are getting ahead of him. For instance, if you're going to push someone out of a window, don't do it in the winter when there's enough snow to break the fall." I suspected Stuart had done the calculations on the way down.

I thought about Percy. A life of one accident after another. "Listen, I have something to tell you. I've got Gareth back in the car. There is no case of a missing scholar for Tristan to solve. That archeologist who disappeared? It was Gareth.

He's Magnus Einarsson. His work wasn't turning out, and rather than let it be known that he'd made a bit of a fool of himself, he changed his name and turned himself into someone else. There was no murder, unless you count Percy. But why kill him?"

"While I was lying here waiting for you to show up, I think I figured it out," Stuart said. "Percy said he had something to tell you, right?"

I'd almost forgotten that. "Yes."

"All right. Tristan must have suspected there was never any missing archeologist. But by then, he was so invested in the story, he decided to manufacture the details. He needed a murderer. Think about it: A body under the rocks with a causeway built over it would never be recovered. The only possible witness around—or, more to the point, one who could verify that none of this had happened—had to go. Percy being out of the picture would clear the way for all indications to point to a researcher, now a respected scholar himself, who may have committed a murder decades ago. I mean, it's the stuff good stories are made of."

My mind was racing. "And very good listener numbers?" I asked. "The best way for Tristan to make sure he could speak *for* Percy was for Percy to be unable to speak for himself. You can't solve a cold case if there is no case. Nothing to be 'solved and resolved.'"

"Speaking of cold ..." Stuart got to his knees, then his feet, and put out a hand. "Maybe we should get inside and warm up. Track down Wade and tell him all of this."

At that moment, the lights went back on, and the pink neon sign of the Peking Restaurant resumed its flashing. As Stuart and I turned to make our way back to the street,

I paused to look back at the outlines of two angels in the snow.

We were quite a pair.

When Stuart and I reached my truck, we found Gareth inside, warm, cozy, and fast asleep. It appeared that Wade, who should have arrived like the cavalry before Stuart was thrown out of the window, had passed us by. If he was out on the highway, giving out a speeding ticket, he and I would have words.

The blast of cold air when we opened the truck door woke Gareth up.

"Did I miss anything?" he asked, startled, a man who had missed most of a lifetime living under an assumed name. He looked us over. "What happened to you two? You're covered in snow."

I pried my phone out of his hand and dialed Wade's cell number. It went to voicemail. "It's winter," I said, too tired to go into the whole story. "You were right about Tristan. He went after Stuart but got away." Stuart walked around to the driver's door of the truck. I should have been bothered that he was taking charge of the driving, but I didn't mind.

"They'll get him," I said, without conviction.

Gareth nodded. He was fading fast from the tension and excitement. I recognized in him a person like I was: one who wanted to be home, have a bath and a tea, and go right to bed. I opened the back door and climbed into the truck's compact back seat, pushing aside Toby's dog blanket. My poor dog. He would be waiting. The evening had gotten away from me.

Stuart looked past Gareth to me. "How about we get everyone back to Gasper's?"

"Thank you," Gareth said. He paused. "Did Valerie tell you who I really am?"

"We didn't have time for a full discussion," Stuart said, cautiously steering back onto the road. "But I got the gist, Magnus."

From where I sat behind him, I could see the old archeologist's shoulders relax with relief. I wasn't sure if it was because he heard his name or because he didn't have to explain again that night what he'd done.

The three of us drove silently through Drummond and onto the one open lane of the causeway. The traffic control crews had been replaced by portable flashing lights and well-lit "Proceed with Caution" signs. When we exited onto the island, I looked over at the store on Front Street. It was well-lit and would be warm.

"After we take Gareth home, maybe you can drop me off at the store. The roads are better, and it's not far home. I'd like to pick up my own car. You can take the truck home, and Duck and I will come over and pick it up in the morning," I said, leaning forward and putting my mitten on Stuart's shoulder.

"You sure?" Stuart asked. "Okay, but go right home. It's been a long day." He didn't say anything else because he didn't have to. Both of us, I knew, were thinking of Tristan and wondering where he was now.

"Kay!" I said. The fear that had been with me most of the evening returned in full force. "What if he's gone to see her?" The podcaster had come to Gasper's Cove with my daughter. Who else did he have to turn to if he was in trouble? We were on the Shore Road now, close to the Inn, but driving in a direction away from Darlene's house.

"Call her," Stuart ordered. "Now."

I scanned through the recent-calls list on my phone for a shortcut for my daughter's number and pressed call.

I waited four rings, then five.

"Kay Rankin's phone." The voice was familiar, but I couldn't place it. "Who am I speaking to?"

"Her mother," I said. "Where's Kay? Who are you?"

"Officer Blanford." I made the connection. This was the junior officer I had seen with Wade. I saw Stuart's eyes flash in the rearview mirror, looking back at me.

"The RCMP?" My throat was tight. I choked on the words. "What has happened to my daughter?"

CHAPTER TWENTY-SEVEN

"Hey, Mom." It was Kay. "Sorry, I was giving a statement. Do you believe this?"

I didn't know what to say to that. I didn't believe anything that had happened for weeks, much less this evening.

"Are you okay?" I asked when I could speak again. "Tristan didn't get to you."

"Tristan? Mom, what are you talking about? The Mounties have taken him in to talk. I don't know why. They won't say, but they want to know how well I know him and what I know about his movements the last few days." I could hear the worry in my daughter's voice. "Do you know what's going on?"

Lots, I thought, but I didn't know where to start. The main thing was that Kay was safe. "He didn't get to you?" I repeated the statement as a question. "They caught him?"

"Mom, you're not making any sense. No one is. But yes, they picked Tristan up. It was actually an Airedale terrier."

"An Airedale?" We had arrived at the Inn. Stuart was out and around, helping Gareth out of the truck. I stayed where I was to talk to Kay.

"Yes. You know how they are," my veterinarian daughter continued. "From what I understand, Tristan was running down the street, and some guy was out walking his dog. It went for his ankle. You know how any kind of terriers are with anything that moves."

I did. The breed was raised to root out rats. This made sense. "Good for the terrier," I said.

"Mom, don't say that. The dog chased him into the road, and Tristan nearly got hit by the snowplow. The operator got scared and called Wade."

I looked out the truck window and saw the front door of the Inn open. Stuart had one arm around Gareth's shoulders and the other hand on his arm, helping the professor up the steps. I saw Catherine outlined in the light and Simon beside her. The black hen in Simon's arms leaned her scrawny neck forward to get a better look at the action on the porch, not wanting to miss anything.

"Listen, Stuart and I are at Rollie and Catherine's, dropping Gareth off. It's a long story. We can be at your place in ten minutes. We can talk."

"No, Mom, it's okay. Don't bother. Officer Blanford is going to take me over to the detachment. Wade wants to see me. I want to see Tristan if I can. There's some kind of mix-up. Maybe I can help straighten it out."

I opened my mouth to tell her not to bother and to suggest she avoid all contact with Tristan for the rest of her life, which shouldn't be too hard since he was undoubtedly on his way to prison. I closed it. My daughter was with the

RCMP. She was safe. I'd let the professionals take it from here.

The truck's door opened. Stuart was back.

"All right then," I said to my daughter. "If you need me, you know where I am." I swallowed. "Kay, I love you."

"Love you, too, Mom."

I put my phone back in my pocket. Stuart climbed into the truck and reached down to move the seat back a few more inches. "Why don't you come in the front with me?" he asked. "How's Kay?"

I got out and then moved in to sit beside Stuart. "Fine, I guess. The RCMP are talking to her. They've already got Tristan." I reached forward and wiped the foggy inside of the windshield with my mitt. Stuart turned the front defroster on to high. "An Airedale terrier caught him."

"I'm not even going to ask," Stuart said.

"How was Gareth?" I asked.

"Tired, overwhelmed, I'd say. Not to worry, Catherine took over. He'll be fine." Stuart reached over and took my hand. "We all will, you know."

Well, not quite, I thought. I wondered how long it would take for the RCMP to get Tristan to tell them where he'd put the body of the Treasure Trovers' president. I took off my damp mitt and squeezed Stuart's hand. It felt cold. "After you drop me off at the store, you should go home too. I am sure Birdie will want to get out." Animals, I thought. Their needs and routines were anchors in the messy lives we humans lived. For that, and a hundred other reasons, we owed them.

"You're right," Stuart said. "I should get back to him. If he gets anxious, he eats shoes."

I laughed, and that felt good. When we arrived at the front of the store and I opened my door, Stuart didn't let go of my hand. Instead, he pulled me closer and kissed me.

"See you later, snow angel."

I took off my other mitt and handed the pair to Stuart. "Put these on," I ordered. "It's a cold night." And it was, but I wasn't.

My car was where I'd left it, in front of the store. I was about to unlock the door and drive home when I remembered the tin of Colleen's oatcakes on the desk in my office. After a day like today, I needed them. I found the store key on my ring and turned the lock to the big front door.

I crossed the threshold, switched on the full row of lights, and walked down the main aisle to my office. Ahead of me, at the landing to the stairs to the basement, I saw Shadow crouched low, her ears up and alert, her haunches ready to jump.

"Hunting for mice?" I asked the cat. I certainly hoped so. I had avoided the basement for weeks, convinced I heard rustling down there. It also seemed to me that every time I picked up the cat, she felt heavier in my arms. I hated mice and was glad she was catching them.

Shadow tensed. She jumped down the steps.

She'd heard something. So had I.

The sound of an ancient toilet flushing, followed by running water.

There was more than a mouse in that basement, and it was walking toward the stairs.

I grabbed our best-quality windshield scraper from Aisle 4, held it high above me, and tried to think. Was this enough? What if whoever was in the basement came up and attacked me before I could defend myself with the scraper? I reached to a shelf behind me, grabbed a yellow hard hat, and pushed it down over the wool hat on my head. I needed more protection. I scanned Aisle 3. There it was, exactly what I needed.

A plastic sled, one of the ones we sold to pull along toddlers. It was perfect. I picked a red one up, looped the yellow plastic rope around my neck for security, and held the sled in front of me like a shield. Armed and protected, padded in my snow jacket and winter boots, ready to kick my way out of any altercation, I felt like a warrior queen, a Norse goddess ready to defend her dependents and her kingdom (in this case, a general store on a forgotten island off Nova Scotia, sundries on the main floor, quilted placemats and thrummed mittens on Level 2).

“Hey,” I yelled. That was a good start. “I know you’re down there. Who are you?”

I pressed my red sled to my chest and raised my windshield scraper even higher. I was down to my last nerve. I’d had enough nonsense for one day. I waited.

And then I heard footsteps on the stairs. Slow steps, pausing on each tread, as if the climber was listening to me as hard as I was listening to them.

The door cracked open wider. I held my breath and my sled tight. The door slowly, slowly, moved open.

There was no one there.

I looked down and saw Shadow as she strolled into the store.

"Shadow!" I relaxed. And then, I realized the cat was not alone.

Right behind her, on the last step, was someone I knew and had not forgotten. He moved one step forward. I moved one step back.

"Hello, Valerie," he said, pausing to take in my warrior princess get-up and holding a hand out toward my windshield scraper. "It's just me. You can take it easy now."

CHAPTER TWENTY-EIGHT

I didn't hand over my weapon. I wasn't about to leave myself defenseless, alone with a dead man.

Not without an explanation. And it'd better be a good one.

"Percy Skinner," I breathed the words out slowly. If I hadn't had the sled to hold up, I would have put my hands on my hips. "Why aren't you dead?"

Percy looked down at his hands to confirm he was still on this earth.

"Because I don't want to be, I guess." He shrugged in a nonchalant way that made me want to bonk him over the head with the sled.

"But you disappeared. Everyone thought you'd been stabbed and dumped into the sea." It felt awkward saying this to the man's face. "Or left under the snow somewhere. 'Til spring."

Percy looked offended, then his face lit up unexpectedly, as if I had jiggled some loose wire in his head and made a connection. "People missed me?" he asked.

"Of course they did. Everyone was worried. How did you get over here, anyway?"

"You brought me."

"What?" Percy wasn't going to pin this on me.

"Sure. I went along for the ride, and when you got here, I decided to hop out. I ducked down to the basement when you were in your office. I needed time to think. I figured it was time to lay low and let him cool down." Percy had the matter-of-fact air of someone who had only done what any normal person would have.

"Him?" I asked. "You mean Tristan?"

Percy stared at me. Shadow pushed herself in front of Toby to rub her body on Percy's legs. "Do you mean that young fellow who makes no sense? What does he have to do with anything?"

It was my turn to stare.

"He's the one who tried to kill you, remember?" I lifted the ring of rope from around my neck and lowered the sled. I sat down on the stack of road-salt bags.

"Tristan? The kid who's always trying to shove a phone in your face?" Percy asked. "The one who came out to my place and tried to get me to talk about the job on the causeway that went wrong years ago? Pushy so-and-so. He had some stupid idea that there were Viking rocks in the fill, and even a dead body. I told him he was crazy, and he said he'd get the evidence somewhere else and left. No, my only problem was Danny."

"Danny?" My head hurt. "What do you mean?"

"Old Danny came out that night when the other guys went in and dragged me off to the end of the parking lot. He was all worked up about those artifacts in his display case.

It was snowing pretty heavy by then. You didn't need to be a genius to know a storm was coming in. Anyway, Danny had a stone bowl thing in his hand and some kind of an old fishing knife. The bowl I didn't mind, but the knife kind of worried me. I was wrong about that. The bowl was made of some kind of heavy stone—you know, the ones they use to pound them spices?"

"Mortar and pestle?"

"Whatever you say," Percy said. "I used to be a meatloaf and mashed potatoes guy myself, but this spicy stuff grows on you. Ever have that vindaloo? Hits the spot on a cold day."

"We can talk about food later," I said. "Keep going. What happened next?"

Percy picked up Shadow. "Danny started talking about this World Heritage scheme he's got going, and I laughed at him. I told him that me and the Trovers had a look at his cabinet and thought it was a joke. That load of old junk would fool no one, especially an experienced group like us. I told him that the only real object of value in the whole region was the rune I found in a yard over in Drummond."

Stuart's lawn ornament. "What did he say to that?"

Percy turned the cat's face around, as if hoping to find sympathy in her yellow eyes before answering me. "That the joke was on me. He told me that stone was probably nothing but something Harry Sutherland had worked up, and the only fool around was me. That did it. I said something that might have been better if I'd kept it to myself."

Talking to Percy Skinner was like searching for artifacts. I tried to keep the impatience out of my voice. "And what was that?"

"I told Danny I had a picture of that stone on my phone. That the first thing I was going to do was send it off to that young reporter fella, Noah, and let everyone know it was a scam. I said, 'Bye-bye, World Heritage Site.' I probably shouldn't have said that," Percy admitted. "But it was a cold night. I wanted to get inside. That's when he did it."

"Did what?"

"Popped me on the nose with the bowl." Percy adjusted the fluorescent tuque he had on his head. I recognized it as one we sold, and he hadn't paid for. "I knocked the knife out of his hand. It fell down into the snow, and I played dead. The doctor's got me on those blood-thinner pills because I got a touch of the A-fib. Blood everywhere. Danny ran off. I didn't feel so good. And I was afraid he'd come back any minute to finish me off. He had an old mallet in that display case, I remembered. The man was not in a good frame of mind. I looked around for somewhere he couldn't find me, until he calmed down." He stopped to contemplate me, as if the next part of the story were my responsibility. "Your truck was right beside me. I hopped in the covered bed in the back, without thinking about it. The rest, you know. I wanted to get out of there. It wouldn't be good for my leadership image for the members to see me in a fight. The Trovers are all I got. I don't talk to anybody else. I had no choice."

With the cat still in his arms, Percy walked over to the pile of sandbags next to the salt and sat down beside me. Shadow purred. He cooed at her as if he had come to the end of his story.

"That's it?" I thought of all the driving I'd done that night. Across the causeway, up to the Inn to drop Gareth off, then back to the store where Stuart had left me to pick up my car.

All that time, I had been driving the truck that Percy had used to make his escape.

"Why didn't you tell me what had happened when we got to the store?" I asked. "Why hide? Why here?" I'd been in my office for a while that night and hadn't locked the back door. I'd do that from now on.

"I was going to," Percy admitted. "I followed you in, but, well, it had been quite a night. The store was warm, it felt safe. I lost my nerve." My indignation must have shown on my face. Percy shifted, nearly slid off the plastic bag, steadied himself, and continued. "It wasn't as if I had any big plan," he said defensively. "I sort of took it as it came. But I got to tell you, it's pretty nice down there. Cozy ... the sounds of people coming and going upstairs. It reminds me of when I was a kid at home, never alone, someone there if you needed them. And there was the cat." Shadow turned up the volume on her purring. They both sighed. "I found a couple of sleeping bags and set myself up behind the furnace. I even heated up coffee in the microwave in your office at night." Percy smiled in remembered contentment. "Then, we had the storm. I couldn't go anywhere anyway. I figured it was only for a few days. I looked around and thought this was good as home, the old trailer. Then, I realized I was wrong: It was better."

It was a lot to take in. The noises I'd heard hadn't been mice—they'd been a man presumed dead. "Let's get this straight. All this time, since that night at the Anchor, you've been living here? What about your jacket? The one they found at the beach?"

Percy stared at me. "They found it? Geez, I'd left it on the back of a chair at the meeting. Someone must have picked it up."

Someone had.

"But doesn't it bother you that the whole of Gasper's Cove thought you were dead?"

"Sure it does," Percy said. "But I didn't know that at the time. I was only giving Danny a chance to settle down while I figured out a way to make it up to him. He had a dream, and I laughed at it. That wasn't right. So, I decided to let it go, the bowl thing. It got out of hand. I don't like people mad at me. And I had the time. And it was warm. ..." His voice trailed off. "You know, that's a good bunch of canning you got down there. And that crock of sauerkraut? I'd say it's just about ready."

While Percy and I waited for the RCMP to arrive, we drank tea, and I tried to talk sense into him. Eventually, I convinced him that since he had been presumed dead, he needed to make an official announcement of his survival. He asked me several times to repeat how the community had been worried about him and exhaled a sigh of relief that I suspected he had held in for at least thirty years. We also solved the mystery of Shadow's sudden weight gain: Percy had been feeding the cat downstairs, while I had been doing the same on the main floor. Her belly had been filled with loving attention, not mice.

I knew, as we talked, that I should have been angrier with Percy than I was. However, I decided I would rather have him annoying than dead. The RCMP was less understanding.

When Wade and Blanford arrived and saw the resurrected Percy, they made it clear to him that the first moral responsibility of any missing person was to let the law know they were not missing at all. But since being alive was not a crime, and since I didn't have it in my heart to accuse Percy of trespassing, in the end, Wade told Percy he was free to go. This didn't make Percy as happy as I thought it would. I caught his longing gaze at the door to the basement and thought of how cold and dark his trailer would be after more than a week of storm and abandonment. That image made up my mind.

It was time Rankin's General acquired a night watchman, and Shadow, an assistant.

That decided, I followed Wade and Blanford to the front of the store and asked about Tristan.

"What happened?" I asked. "Gareth told the detachment that you should go to Stuart's office and arrest Tristan for murder. But you drove right by."

"I know you always think you are running every investigation"—Wade gave me a look—"but by the time I got that message, we were already on our way to pick him up. He's wanted for questioning about a case across the pond. A plow operator called in about a man running down the middle of the road. ... A dog got him first."

"Where is he now?" I asked.

"The other car took him to the station, and we came over here," Wade said. "We'll take a statement, hold him until someone comes to get him. We don't want him. Since he's from overseas, they can deal with the issue of what he did to Stuart and attempted murder in Halifax. It's going to get complicated. He's made trouble here, but that's all."

I wondered what Kay would think. It could have been worse. At least now I didn't need to tell her I'd never liked her friend. That was one conversation that would be better left unsaid.

"There was no murder, was there?" I asked. "Not years ago, and not now?"

"You mean the professor? We know about that, and it seems Percy's turned up. Alive. Not dead is always a good thing in our business," Wade said. "It looks like all we got here was greed and ego. I don't know what to call the rest of it."

"I do," I said. "Too many people trying to be someone or something they're not. That always catches up with a person."

And in all cases, it had.

CHAPTER TWENTY-NINE

The night before Kay flew back to Scotland, alone, Darlene, George, and Duck arrived back from Cuba.

They all looked tanned, well rested, and glad to be home.

"We had a fine time," Darlene said, when she dropped off Kay to stay with me for her last evening, "but to be honest, we felt we were missing all the excitement. An all-inclusive resort's pretty dull when you're used to Gasper's Cove. We spent most of the time at the beach on our phones, trying to keep up."

I believed this. "Funny you ran into Duck," I said. "How was that?"

"Great," Darlene said. "I mean, George and I knew each other, but what kind of holiday would Duck have had by himself? I mean, who does that?" No one we knew.

After Darlene left, Kay and I had dinner together one last time before she returned to her own life. Pressured by time at the same table slipping away, I decided to broach the subject of Tristan the only way I knew how.

"How are you doing?" I asked. "With all of this that's been going on?"

"You mean, do I feel like a loser? Because I brought home someone I didn't really know?" Kay took our plates to the sink and rinsed them off with surgical care.

"Something like that," I admitted. And, because I was her mother, I had to add, "You're not the loser, he is."

"Thanks, Mom," Kay smiled. This was a good sign. "I think you said the same thing to me in Grade 7." She opened the cupboard, took out some mugs, filled the kettle, and plugged it in. "It wasn't a surprise to me, to tell you the truth. He was all over me when he found out I was from Nova Scotia, but once we were here, I never saw him. It felt weird, the way he chatted everyone up, like he was taking advantage of the fact they were polite. I was embarrassed. It's not like we are some kind of artifact to turn over and examine." I knew what she meant.

We sat there together for a moment. To break the silence, I asked, "What time is your flight?" I wondered when I would see her again.

"In the afternoon, Mom. But not to worry, I have a ride to the airport." Kay lifted the lid of my big brown teapot and studied the inside of it, avoiding my eyes.

"You do?"

"Yes. Noah. He says he's got something going on in Halifax, going there anyway." She turned around from the counter with a don't-ask-anymore-questions look on her face. "We're having lunch before I go, with a friend I know from vet school. Someone with a new practice in Drummond," she added.

"Great," I said. A vet friend here? I pretended I wouldn't extract hope from this news.

But Kay had learned her topic-changing skills from her mother. She picked up her mug and set it down. "You know, we all like Stuart," she said. "A lot." She sat. "Remember when you told me to hold out for the real thing?"

I nodded.

"It was good advice. Maybe you should take it."

Kay was a real Rankin. We always had the last word.

The next morning, after Noah and Kay drove away, the house seemed too empty to stay in. So, I grabbed Toby and his leash and headed up to the Shore Road in the car.

The snow had stopped, and the day was so bright, I had to stop and put my sunglasses on. Here on the coast, a storm could retreat as fast as it came. As I drove, I could already see the warm weather had started to melt the snow on rooftops, sliding giant slabs onto what and whoever was below. When Toby and I arrived at the Inn, I noted the giant icicle hanging from the eaves and moved away from under it. The Inn was quiet. I glanced over at the patio. The chicken coop looked abandoned.

Catherine opened the door.

"Kay's gone, has she?" Catherine said, seeing my face, knowing immediately how I felt. "She'll be back," she added, also knowing what I needed to hear.

"Let's hope so," I said. My daughter had checked herself twice in the mirror when Noah's car had pulled up in front of the house.

I followed Catherine inside. My cousin's plaid jacket and boots were missing from the hook and tray at the front entry. "Where's Rollie?" I asked.

"He's driven Gareth to the bus," she said. "He pulled a few strings and got Gareth hired to teach online at the university. It's a job Gareth can do from home. Rollie figures it will do him good to be back in the classroom, but in a way that will be easier on him."

"He'll like that," I said. "That man is born to lecture." I remembered the Inn's other winter guest. "How about Simon? Is he still working on his book?"

Catherine held up her finger to her mouth to shush me and pulled me into the alcove she had set up as the Inn's library.

"He's still here, but I wouldn't mention the book," she said.

"Why not?" I asked.

"The publisher looked at the first chapters and withdrew the contract offer. They said it didn't have the 'same voice' they'd seen in the proposal."

"Poor Simon. He must have been devastated."

"He was," Catherine said. "You have no idea. He dragged himself around here like he'd lost the will to live." She smiled, which I thought was unsympathetic. "Then, the girls stepped in." She turned her head and looked down the hall. "There they are now."

And they were.

The door to the bathroom opened, and Simon came out. He had on the same loose, too short, too cinched-in corduroy pants and outsized flannel shirt he'd worn when we met.

What was missing was his phone, the notebook, and the stress on his face.

"Hey, Val," he said, "what's happening?" He ambled down toward me.

He was not alone.

Following behind him, like a gaggle of nervous mothers watching an unreliable toddler, were five hens.

"It is insane," Catherine said in a stage whisper. "The lower Simon got, the closer the girls moved in. Now, they don't let him go anywhere without them."

"You're talking about the *chickens*?"

"You got it," Catherine said, quickly. "If you're lucky, you'll be here when he sits down and one of them starts grooming his head."

"I see you have fans," I said when Simon and the chickens were closer.

He looked down at his feet. "We're a bit of a unit," he said. "They need me. We've bonded. That will be easier when we move."

"Move?" I asked. Beside me, Catherine studied her ceiling.

"Yes," Simon said, picking up the fattest and reddest hen. "I've found a place down the road to rent. Lots of space for me and my ladies. They need their own home, something more predictable than a place with people coming and going. And"—he cleared his throat—"I've met a woman. An academic who has her own birds. ..." He smiled and looked at his charges. "I'm changing directions."

"In what way?" I asked. "Apart from the chickens."

Simon put the hen down, as if to spare her ears news of his previous life. "All those books I worked on were starting to get to me," he explained. "Every time I wrote about the zombie apocalypse, I started to wonder: Did I have the skills to survive that sort of end-of-the-world scenario? Alone?" His eyes looked huge behind his thick glasses. "The obvious answer was no. I grew up in Brooklyn. I knew if I couldn't order in, I would starve. I've never lived without taxis, steam facials, or my therapist. What would I do? That's why I came here. To learn how to manage. And you taught me it wasn't necessary."

"Not sure I follow," I said.

"The key to surviving is to not try to do it alone. The only real prepping anyone needs is other people they can count on." Simon stroked the chicken like it was a cat. "Does that make sense?"

It did. Completely. "What now?"

"We'll see what I'll work on next. It might be time to find a new publisher and a new audience." Simon watched one of his girls peck at the fringe on Catherine's antique rug. "The main thing"—he looked up and beamed at me—"is I found my flock."

Later that week, I had a chance to watch Stuart bake. I'd never seen anything like it. My own method involved old measuring cups bought a generation ago at some Tupperware party, the quantities long worn off, the half cup missing after it had gone into a sandpile once and never come back.

Stuart weighed his ingredients.

"Two hundred and eighty-four grams," he announced, leaning down to read the display on the digital scale on the counter. He carefully added the flour into a bowl with 110 grams of packed brown sugar.

I talked to his back.

“I meant to tell you, I solved the mystery of the weather report,” I said. “It was neither a technical nor human problem.”

The word *technical* got Stuart’s attention. He turned and wiped his hands on the tea towel hanging over the oven door. I was proud of my topstitching on his apron—straight as a die. The ledge on the edge-stitching foot was my secret weapon.

“What do you mean?” he asked.

“When Noah picked up Kay, he told me. He knows someone at Environment Canada who worked on the meteorological software. When they decided to go modern, CKGC bought an earlier version, something called a beta, before the bugs were worked out.”

Stuart rolled his eyes. “Why doesn’t this surprise me?”

I continued, trying my best to be as precise as I could be. “They got a deal,” I explained. “Early AI. You know what that is?”

“Artificial intelligence,” Stuart answered, waiting for me to continue.

“Right, not as good as real intelligence, at least not the beta model,” I said. “You know how our Internet goes down all the time during a storm?”

“Sure do, no excuse.”

No argument there. “Anyway, when the software was unable to get the current readings up on the cloud, wherever that is, the not-so-intelligent software reverted to the last readings. Most of which were leftovers from better weather.” I loved this part of the story, it was so CKGC. “And that’s what they broadcasted.”

Stuart laughed. "So, what are they going to do now? Upgrade? Get a better server?"

I was ready for this question. Noah had explained that to me too. "Nope. They're going back to traditional weather forecasting. Look out the window, watch for how low the birds are flying, study the waves. The animals know first what's going to happen." A memory came back to me. "That's what my dad always said."

Stuart opened his oven door to check the round thermometer he had hanging on one of the racks. He told me he didn't always trust factory-set readings on the stove. The right temperature mattered.

"Sometimes, progress isn't all it's cracked up to be," he muttered, putting on the oven mitts I'd made to go with the apron. I was eating so much of his cooking these days, sewing him something to wear while he did it seemed the least I could do.

The mention of progress reminded me of the manager of the Anchor Motel.

"You know Danny's scheme to get this place designated as a World Heritage Site?" I asked. "The one Harry custom-made a rune for at the beginning of this whole saga?"

"How could I forget?" Stuart unrolled parchment paper onto a cookie sheet. "Remember, I'm the one Tristan tried to get to sign off on the idea of a rune, and maybe a body, under the causeway."

"Exactly, how could I forget?" No, I would never forget how I felt standing at the open window in the dark, looking down and seeing Stuart lying motionless in the snow. "And in the end, there was nothing there."

Stuart took off one of his oven mitts and rubbed his chin, as if considering what to say next. "No," he said finally. "You're right. That was just a myth. But have you heard the latest? The deal Danny and Percy made? It was Gareth's idea."

"A deal? Danny hit Percy on the nose with a bowl. What kind of deal would those two make?"

"The one a guy like Danny would come up with so Percy wouldn't press charges," Stuart said. "Danny bought him off."

"He did? How?"

"Like I said, Gareth's idea. When he told Danny his collection was worthless, he tried to soften the blow by pointing out that more people visit Ripley's Believe It or Not! every year than many museums. That gave Danny the idea to hire Percy and Harry to come up with *Are they real, or aren't they?* treasures. He figures there is more money to be made personally from a 'Wonders of the World' display than from being a little motel in a World Heritage Site."

I thought this over. Maybe it was better to keep our heritage the way it was and let the sensation seekers have what they could appreciate most. I noticed the smile had faded from Stuart's face.

"What's wrong?" I asked. "There's something else, isn't there? That you're not telling me."

"You're right," Stuart admitted. "It's about that inspection I did on the causeway. I haven't told anyone this, but a few other things turned up during that storm that make me uneasy."

"Like what?" I asked. Birdie sat up under the table, his Duck Toller's ears wide like propellers, alert for the hunt.

Stuart walked over and sat down with me at the kitchen table. "It's a long story. Something's not right with how the municipality is spending money. It's going to take checking out, but without anyone knowing I'm behind it, for professional reasons. I'm not sure what to do."

I reached over and took Stuart's hand.

"Not to worry," I said. "What you need is someone with a lot of hobbies, someone no one would take seriously, someone no one will notice, who could get in and find out what you need."

Stuart smiled at me. "You mean, I need a sewing teacher?"

"Sort of, but I'm thinking more like an investigator, a partner, on an ongoing basis. Semipermanent. Or permanent. What do you think?"

"What I think," Stuart said, reaching behind his neck to take off his apron, "is that that is exactly who I need."

Under the table, Birdie nudged my knee with his nose.

"Excellent," I said. "So, when do we start?"

THE END

READER'S GUIDE

Crafting an Alibi

BY BARBARA EMODI

1. At one point, Valerie notes, "As a sewing teacher and crafter, I knew how to see the possibilities others might miss in otherwise-ordinary materials." Do you feel that is accurate? Do your pastime activities inform your outlook on life events?

2. Danny assumes that tourists will flock to the area in part because portions of the area are mainly undeveloped. He notes that tourists flocked to a similar area because "The place looks like it did 300 years ago. That's all. No progress." Do you think that is true? Have you ever visited a location because it was undeveloped?

3. Valerie notes that to tourists, "[E]verything we'd done to make do was the work of artisans, even art." Can you think of any similar examples in your own region? Have you ever purchased anything solely because it was made traditionally?

4. Valerie pontificates that visitors to Gasper's Cove are "refugees from prosperity who wanted to connect with a simpler way of life they had never personally experienced." Can you think of a tourist area that resembles this statement? Are you attracted to these types of vacation destinations?

5. The area of Nova Scotia where the fictional Gasper's Cove is located is steeped in tradition, which is often reflected in odd sayings. Colleen notes that "the year of the white mice" translates to "a long time ago." Are there any similar sayings that are specific to your region? Do you remember any of your older family members using similar regionalisms?

6. Several points in the story contrast how differently people view challenging circumstances now than they did in the past. In this story, those views are often centered around the weather. Are there things that you would have done as a matter of course as a child that would now be viewed as dangerous?

7. When attending sewing class, Simon is astonished by how much the locals are able to make rather than buy—for example, cheese. Is there something that your parents or grandparents routinely made that you would never dream of tackling? Do you regret not having these skills?

8. In years past, some items or shops were inaccessible during certain seasons or conditions. One character notes that she keeps a "death ham" on hand, just in case. Is there anything you remember you, your parents, or grandparents keeping on hand for unexpected events or circumstances?

9. At one point, Simon brings up that it is believed that Al Capone used to visit the area. What famous people are from or visited your hometown? Was it a well-known fact or something that could score a point at the next trivia contest?

10. Valerie notes, "Some of us are made to have our palates cleansed. And others of us are born to wipe donair sauce from our chins." What do you think she means by this? Do you think it is true?

11. The harsher aspects of the climate are a focus of this book, and they show how this aspect of the geography has shaped the people who live there. Valerie notes, "I sometimes wondered if there would be any Gasper's Cove crafters without winter." How has climate or geography shaped the area where you live?

12. Valerie notes, "To us, a storm day could be a gift." Are there any instances you can think of where something that would likely be a negative to many is a positive to you?

13. The nature of small towns plays a factor in all the Gasper's Cove mysteries. While this can be a double-edged sword, Valerie wonders if "not having those connections left a vacancy in a soul that would make a new identity plausible." Do you feel that change or reinvention is impossible in a small community? Is that a positive or a negative?

14. In this story, Stuart tells Valerie that he knew she'd understand his cryptic message. Do you feel this is a shift in his attitude toward Valerie?

15. Valerie notes, "I should have been bothered that [Stuart] was taking charge of the driving, but I didn't mind." Do you feel this shows progress in her relationship with Stuart?

16. In the past, Valerie has had difficulty trusting that her children will be able to resolve their own problems. In this story, she refrains from jumping in, noting, "My daughter was with the RCMP. She was safe. I'd let the professionals take it from here." Do you think this was difficult for her?

17. For once, Val actually solves one of the mysteries—who stole the snowplow. Does this show growth on her part or luck?

18. Pets feature heavily in this series. Valerie notes, "Their needs and routines were anchors in the messy lives we humans lived. For that, and a hundred other reasons, we owed them." Do you agree with this statement? How have your pets, past or present, improved your life?

19. Valerie notes that Stuart's dog, Birdie, is "well insulated, both by his waterproof coat and by every dog's conviction that today was the best day of his life." Do you think it is possible for people to have that same sense of optimism?

20. An overarching theme of this book is authenticity. Valerie states that trying to be someone or something they are not always catches up with a person. Have you ever tried to be something you are not? Do you feel that being inauthentic does always catch up to you?

21. Community is a central theme in this series. In this book, Simon learns that the key to survival is to learn to count on others. Is this a true statement for you personally?

22. Simon's character changes throughout this book. In the end, he seems more content because, as the character states, "I found my flock." Do you think that people with a strong social circle are more content? Can you think of times when this may and may not be true?

23. In a way, Gareth has to return to Gasper's Cove to regain his sense of self. If there was one time or place you could return to, what would it be, and why?

24. Irony plays a large role in this book. Gareth and Percy are, for different reasons, examples of irony. Gareth authenticates items, but he is living under a false identity. Percy spends so much time searching for items, only to vanish himself. Can you think of any other instances of irony in this story?

25. Colleen says to Valerie, "You don't borrow someone else's life. You write your own." What do you think she means by that? Is it okay to immerse yourself in another culture?

26. Artificial intelligence, or lack thereof, plays a part in this story. In the instance of the weather station, the technology is faulty. Do you think that AI has a part in our society?

27. "Progress," Simon observes, "isn't always what it's cracked up to be." Do you agree with his statement? Can you think of times when things that were meant to be a positive step forward were actually anything but?

28. Valerie expresses skepticism regarding artificial intelligence. She notes that removing the human element does not guarantee progress. Do you think that AI needs human checks and balances?

29. Gareth plays a role in unraveling the mystery in part because he is disregarded in some situations. Do you think this is due to his age or his personality?

ABOUT THE AUTHOR

Barbara Emodi lives and writes in Halifax, Nova Scotia, Canada, with her husband, a rescue dog, and a cat, who all appear in her writing in various disguises. She has grown children and grandchildren in various locations and, as a result, divides her time between Halifax and the United States so no one misses her too much.

Barbara has published two sewing books—*SEW: The Garment-Making Book of Knowledge*, and *Stress-Free Sewing Solutions*, and she is a course instructor on the innovative and interactive platform Creative Spark Online Learning (by C&T Publishing). In another life, she has been a journalist, a professor, and a radio commentator.

To keep in touch with Barbara, sign up for her newsletter through her website: **babsemodi.com**

And follow her Substack column, How to Be an Older Woman for Beginners.

To keep up with Barbara, sign up for her newsletter through the link on her website. Visit Barbara online and follow on social media!

Website: babsemodi.com

Instagram: @bemodi

TikTok: @babsemodi

Fiction website: babsemodi.com

Creative Spark: creativespark.ctpub.com

Gasper's Cove Mysteries Series

ANN HAZELWOOD
QUILTERS of the DOOR
First Novel in the DOOR COUNTY QUILTS Series

the Basement QUILT
a novel by
Ann Hazelwood
Introducing the Colebridge Community

FIRST NOVEL IN THE EAST PERRY COUNTY SERIES
ANN HAZELWOOD
THE FORGIVING QUILT

Ann Hazelwood
For the LOVE of QUILTS
First novel in the Wine Country Quilts Series

2nd edition includes instructions to make the featured quilt
Tie Died
a quilting cozy
Carol Dean Jones

GASPER'S COVE MYSTERIES BOOK 1
CRAFTING FOR MURDER
BARBARA EMODI

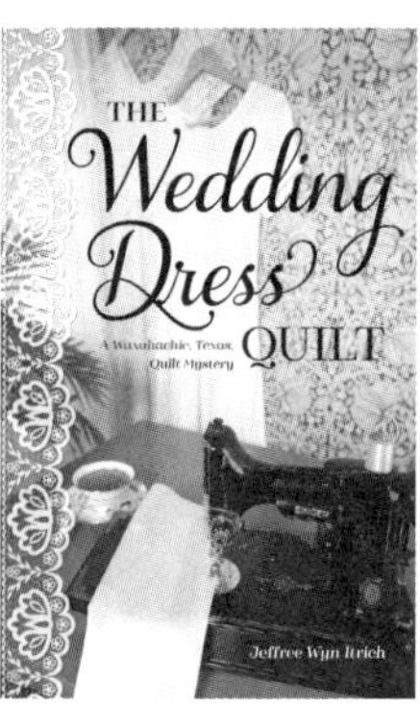

THE Wedding Dress QUILT
Jeffree Wyn Itrich